whiteout

Dan Bomkamp

Lovstad Publishing
Poynette, Wisconsin
Lovstadpublishing@live.com

ISBN: 0692491023
ISBN-13: 978-0692491027
Previous ISBN: 0615752098

Printed in the United States of America

Books by Dan Bomkamp
The Adventures of Thunderfoot
More Adventures of Thunderfoot
Thanks, Thunderfoot
The Gosey
Big Edna
Voyageur
Lost Flight
Tag
Spirit

Cover design by Lovstad Publishing
Cover photo by Dan Bomkamp

DEDICATION

This book is dedicated to my Dad. He opened my eyes to the wonders of the great outdoors. How I wish we could have shared more of it together.

Acknowledgements

I want to thank Mike Valley of Valley Fish Market in Prairie du Chien, Wisconsin for the information on commercial fishing. He was gracious enough to take the time to answer my many questions and gave me some good stuff for the book.

Thanks also to my Publisher, fellow author and friend, Joel Lovstad, for his help with all of my books and his expertise in putting them together for me.

I want to thank Rafael Hakim, Brandon Maloney and Dylan Maloney for portraying my characters, Julio, Noah and Sebastian on the cover.

whiteout

"The outdoors holds many things of keen delight. A deer flashing across a burn, a squirrel corkscrewing up a tree trunk, a sharp tail throbbing up from the stubble... all these have their place in my scheme of things. But the *magic visitation* of ducks from the sky to a set of bobbing blocks holds more beauty and heart-pounding thrill than I have ever experienced afield with rod or gun. Not even the sure hard pluck of a hard-to-fool brown trout or the lurching smash of a river smallmouth has stirred me as has the circling caution of ducks coming to decoys."

Gordon MacQuarrie
Stories of the Old Duck Hunters and other Drivel

whiteout

CHAPTER 1

Autumn 1940

I COULD HEAR VOICES coming from downstairs and knew that my best friend Noah Pederson was arguing with my grandma like they did every time they were together.

"What do you mean Danish Vikings? There were no Danish Vikings. All Vikings were Norwegians, not those dumb Danes," Grandma said.

"What? Have you forgotten about Eric the Red? He was one of the most famous Vikings in history and he was a Dane."

"Eric the Red," the old woman scoffed. "He was nothing but a fairytale."

Gram was a died-in-the-wool Norwegian and the idea that someone other than a Norwegian had been a Viking was just not acceptable to her. Of course Noah took every opportunity to poke fun at the old woman.

I had to grin as I listened to them. Noah's real grandmother had died when he was a little kid and he'd just adopted my grandma as his Gram too. We've been friends since we were in diapers and have spent most of our lives together up our present sixteen year age. Soon I heard the thumping of Noah's size thirteen socked feet on the stairs as he came to my room.

"Its daylight in the swamp.....time to get up you lazy lout."

"Go away! It's Saturday, a day of rest."

"You have Saturday confused with Sunday my lazy friend," he said as he flopped onto my bed.

"Mmmmmmmuuuueeeaaawwww!" My golden retriever Katy yawned and rolled over as Noah began hugging her and rubbing her belly.

"Kate my love, how are you today?" he said to the dog. Kate turned her head and licked his face.

"She's tired yet, and so am I," I said.

"We've got a lot to do today. Duck season's not far away and I'm not going to freeze my butt off standing in the tall grass trying to hide from the ducks this year. We're going to have a proper duck blind and today we're going to start on it."

"You go ahead and I'll come down later."

He slapped me on the butt and sat up on the bed. "I'll give you three seconds and then I'm going to reach under the blankets and grab your big toe and drag you out."

I shook my head and rolled over on my back. He stood up, towering over my bed with a goofy grin on his face. His hair was sticking out at all angles from wrestling with Katy. I had to smile at him as he stood there looking like a slightly crazy Viking.

Noah is six foot three and built like a lumber jack. He wears his blond hair pretty long and has that wide handsome Danish face that is set off by his ice blue eyes. He turned his head slightly sideways and said, "Don't you with you were as dang handsome as I am? Then you'd get as many girls as I do and I wouldn't have to work so hard to get some extras for you."

"Baloney, I can get all the girls I need without your help. The girls that go out with you do it because they feel pity for you since you're so pathetic."

"Oh yeah?" He said raising his eyebrows. He grabbed my foot and began dragging me out of the bed. Kate jumped up and began barking and wagging her tail.

"Get him Kate! Kill! Go for his throat!" I said to the dog.

Noah just laughed and pulled me out of the bed. "Now get washed up and dressed. Gram has breakfast almost ready."

He patted his leg and Katy ran to him and followed him down the stairs. I sat there on the floor and shook my head. There was never a dull moment with Noah around.

I went into the bathroom and did my morning business and then brushed my teeth. I looked at myself in the mirror and was pretty pleased with what I saw. My hair is darker than Noah's and a bit shorter but otherwise I'm not bad looking. Maybe I'm not drop dead handsome but the girls seem to think I'm ok. I'm about 3 inches shorter than Noah and pretty well built.

"Sebastian, that dumb Dane is going to eat everything if you don't get down here," my grandma called up the stairway.

I went down the stairs to the kitchen where the smell of fresh baked cinnamon rolls filled the room. Gram was scrambling some eggs and a plate of bacon was sitting on the table. Noah was giving Katy a piece of bacon but being careful not to get caught by Gram.

"I told this dummy that it's a waste of time to build a duck blind. The way this fall is going, the ducks won't come down from Canada until the season is over and you guys won't get a chance at any of them...duck blind or no duck blind."

"Oh Gram," Noah said, "don't worry. We men will bring in plenty of ducks for you women-folk so you won't starve this winter. The ducks will come. They always do and this year we'll be ready for them."

"Suddenly you're an expert on duck hunting? You two hunted ducks for the first time last year and I might say were less than successful if I judge by the number of duck dinners we had," Gram said.

"We were just learning the trade," Noah said stuffing half a cinnamon roll in his mouth.

Actually Gram was right our duck season last year was a real mess. We had no idea how or where to hunt and ended up trying to hide in tall grass and shoot at ducks that just happened to fly too close to us. We'd listened to duck hunting stories for years and had hunted squirrels and grouse for several years. We figured duck hunting couldn't be too much more difficult. It turned out that we had no idea what to do or where to do it and our lack of knowledge led us to a pretty unsuccessful season. This year we hoped to improve our success by having a decent blind to hunt from and maybe we'd get a few more ducks.

Gram just shook her head as she put the eggs on the table. "Sit

Sebastian take some food before this barbarian eats it all."

I looked around the kitchen. "Where's Karen?" I asked Noah.

"She stayed down at the boat dock with dad. She was interested in something in the bulrushes and didn't want to walk all the way up here."

Karen is Noah's wire-haired dachshund. She is a typical dachshund with little short legs and a long skinny body but instead of being sleek, her hair is long and mottled gray making her look something akin to a shaggy otter. She thinks she's a water spaniel and swims like a fish. She and Katy are best friends.

"I asked Dad about using the big boat today and he said we can have it all afternoon. He has a couple of strings of fish traps to check this morning so I thought you and I would go along and help him so he gets finished sooner. Then we can spend the day checking out some places for our blind."

I'd never been with them checking hoop nets so I thought it might be kind of fun and surely would be educational. "That sounds ok with me. Do I need anything special to take along?"

"No, we've got some extra rain gear and boots. Dad said we can tear down that old smoker now that the new one is completed too. I figure we'll tear it down and then we can use the wood from it for our blind."

"Seems like you've got it all figured out," I said grinning.

"Of course I do….I'll do all the figuring and all you have to do is supply your brawn and hammer things together where I show you." Noah grinned from ear to ear.

"You two are wasting your time," Grandma said. "Those ducks are all still in Canada and northern Minnesota, they won't come down until after the season is over. You mark my words all you'll be shooting at are wood ducks and a few teal."

Noah grinned. "Those little local ducks will sharpen our shooting eyes Gram. One of these days the weather will turn and then we'll be ready with the best duck blind on the river."

Grandma just shooed at him with her dish towel. "A waste of

time, but who can tell a dumb Dane anything?"

We finished our breakfast and Noah wrapped a slice of bacon in his hanky for Karen and we pulled on our shoes and kissed Gram goodbye and headed down the road to the fish market. Katy was loping along in front of us stopping now and then to sniff a weed or to stray off the road checking out the smells.

"Your Gram sure is a funny old woman," Noah said.

"I think she likes you better than she likes me sometimes," I said.

"She sure likes to argue with me more," he said grinning.

Since Noah's own grandmother died when he was just a baby and he never knew her and since we spent so much time together from our toddler days on, when I started calling my grandmother Gram, he did too. Gram loved the idea of having an extra grandson even though she acted like Noah was the worst pest in the world. They both loved each other and weren't fooling anyone.

We walked down the street past Noah's house and on toward the river. There was a backwater slough that opened to the main channel where Noah's father had built a large boat dock that he used for tying up his commercial fishing boat. The dirt road ran down through the woods to the dock. The family fish market stood on the shore a short walk from the boat landing. Noah's father had built a new smokehouse next to the market so the old one which stood on the riverbank was no longer going to be used and it would make a great duck blind. Noah's dad was puttering around in the boat as we walked up.

"Well, morning Sebastian, and Katy, how are you two this fine morning?"

"Morning sir, we're fine. Nice morning for a boat ride."

Noah's father Steffen was an older version of Noah. He was a big man, well over six feet tall, brown haired but with a few strands of gray showing. He also had a big wide Danish face with piercing blue eyes. I noticed that he too was smiling and very jolly, so early in the morning. "Well boys, let's get out there and see what the river gods gave me in my nets."

I patted the side of the boat and said to Katy, "Hop in Big Kate." The dog jumped over the gunwale of the boat and began sniffing the deck as Noah and I climbed in.

"Where's Karen?" Noah asked.

"Karen....come on girl."

Soon the reeds began rattling as Karen snuffed her way through toward the boat. Katy began to bark as she saw her friend. Noah leaned over the side of the boat and picked the little dog up and put her in the bottom of the boat where she and Katy growled and pawed at each other, play fighting.

Steffen pushed us out from the dock and went to the back of the boat to start the motor. Soon we were off, the morning fog just lifting as we slid through the dark water of the Mississippi river.

CHAPTER 2

STEFFEN PILOTED THE BOAT down through the narrow channel and then out onto the main river. He had to be careful in the narrow confines of the side channels. The boat was 20 feet long and almost 8 feet wide. The bottom was flat and the sides came up at an angle giving great stability which made walking around in it very easy. It was a working boat, made of sturdy wood with an open construction. It had one purpose, to haul boxes of fish from the river.

In the back end of the boat was an enclosure with a gasoline car motor that propelled the boat by a shaft that ran through the transom and connected to a propeller. Steffen steered the boat with a rudder that he ran from just behind the motor enclosure. Noah and I piled a couple of the wooden fish boxes on top of each other and sat on them during the ride. We headed upriver and then Steffen took a side channel to the west and soon he cut the throttle and began slowing down. He watched the riverbank carefully looking for a tiny piece of white cloth that was tied to a branch of an overhanging tree, and soon he nodded to Noah.

Noah and I had put on rubber bibbed pants, rubber jackets and boots and were wearing rubber gloves and we went to the bow of the boat. Noah picked up a large grappling hook which was tied to a rope and dropped it over the front of the boat. When it touched bottom he nodded to his dad and Steffen slowly turned the boat toward the middle of the channel. I watched Noah as he felt the hook dragging on the bottom and suddenly it got heavy. He began to pull on the rope and said, "Got it."

Steffen cut the motor back to idle speed and waited until Noah had the hook to the boat. He took the hook off the rope he had snagged and he and I began to haul the rope up. Within a minute we had the upper end of a large hoop net at the surface.

The hoop net was a long contraption that looked like a big sausage with funnels on each end. It was three and a half feet wide with nine wooden rings spaced throughout its twenty foot length. There was cotton netting stretched over the hoops from end to end making a trap for fish that swam in through either end. At the ends there was a funnel of netting that was widest at the outside end and got progressively narrower toward the inside of the net. The idea was that a fish swam along until he encountered the net and then started inside through the wide opening. As he moved forward the opening got smaller but most of the fish just kept going until they were inside. Once inside, the opening to get out was very small and most of them just stayed put.

The net was anchored at the upper end with a piece of cement block tied to a rope that kept the net in place in the current. It was also anchored at the lower or tail end with another weight, keeping it right where the fisherman left it. As long as you knew where to look along the shore for a marker you could find your nets and didn't have to worry about someone else messing with them. Of course most other fishermen would never touch a fellow fisherman's property but just in case, fishermen didn't advertise where their nets were located.

Noah and I began to lift the net and as we did, the fish in it moved to the lower end which was still down in the water. The more we lifted, the heavier the net got as the fish piled up. Soon we had three quarters of the net out of the water and lying on the bow of the boat. The dogs were very excited to see all the fish thrashing around and Karen began barking at them. When all the fish were in the bottom of the net, Steffen motioned to us to stop lifting.

Then he untied a couple of small ropes that held the last two hoops together and opened the net. Noah went back to help his dad. He set three of the wooden fish boxes in the bottom of the boat. The boxes were three feet square and about one foot high. As they sorted the fish by species they piled them into a box

16

until it was three quarters full and then set another box on top and kept going. One box would hold all the carp, while another was for catfish and the third for assorted species like red horse, blue buffalo, sheep head and ciscoes. Then when they got back to shore, they would shovel ice chips over the fish to keep them fresh.

"A pretty good haul," Steffen said looking at the fish flopping around in the net. He began to grab fish and toss them into the boxes. Noah also began sorting the fish. There were several catfish, many carp, some sheep head and a few buffalo fish. It was a good thing we'd put on the rubber suits or we'd have gotten soaked by the splashing fish. Occasionally they'd come on a bluegill or bass and they tossed them back into the river. It was illegal to keep game fish.

"Wow, look here," Noah said as he held up a nice walleye. "Too bad I couldn't catch this one on my fishing pole. It'd make some good eating."

"Put her back," his dad said grinning. "But don't tell Gram or she'll have a fit."

It didn't take long and the net was empty. Steffen connected the two hoops again and they let it drop back to the bottom of the river. The three fish boxes were each about half full. Noah rinsed off his gloves in the river and then he and I sat back on our boxes and Steffen fired up the motor and we headed upstream to the next net.

"I've been thinking about where to put the blind," Noah said over the whine of the motor.

"Yeah? What did you have in mind?" I asked.

"Well, I want to find a place next to the channel where there's a marsh close by. That way we can get some of those diving ducks that come down late from the north. They stay on the channel and if we've got our blind off in some backwater pond, they'll never come close enough for us to shoot at them. Remember last year? We saw thousands of ducks flying around out over the main river and we didn't get a shot at one of them."

I nodded. "I think that's a good idea," I said. "Plus if it does ever get cold, the backwaters will freeze up and we'll be done hunting. If we have a blind next to the channel, it'll stay open a lot later in the season."

Noah nodded.

We rounded a bend in the channel and Steffen slowed down. Noah got up and went to the bow with the hook and watched his dad. Steffen scanned the riverbank and then saw what he was looking for. "See that tree that the beaver have been chewing? The anchor is straight out from that tree."

Noah watched as the tree got close and then dropped the hook. Steffen turned the boat out toward the middle and Noah immediately snagged the line. I helped him pull it up and soon they were emptying the second net.

We went from net to net and soon had visited all six that were set. We had nearly all of the fish boxes filled with fish and the boat was sitting much lower in the water with all the added weight. Noah and I sat on the edge of a couple of the boxes while the dogs sniffed the fish and watched with great interest. Steffen turned the boat downriver and we headed toward the dock to unload the first part of the days catch.

CHAPTER 3

STEFFEN PULLED THE BOAT up alongside the dock and Noah jumped out and tied it up. Kate jumped onto the dock and I lifted Karen up and the two dogs took off for the cattails. Noah's grandpa Jorgen came down the walkway pushing a flat cart and we began loading boxes of fish onto it. When it was full I helped Jorgen push it back up to the fish house.

Once all the fish were inside the building Steffen said to Noah. "Do you think you and Sebastian can pull the other string of traps? I'd like to stay and help get these fish cleaned and ready for market."

"Sure dad, I know where they are. I'll just watch for the markers. Is that ok with you?" he asked me.

"I'm ok with it. As long as you know where they are I think we can do it." We went back, called the dogs and then loaded up to go back out on the river.

Noah had been with his dad many times checking the fish traps and he knew right where to go. We turned up the correct channel and soon he slowed down looking for the little bit of cloth tied to the first tree. When he saw it he told me to drop the hook. I could feel it sliding across the gravel bottom and soon it began to feel heavy. I lifted and could feel the weight of the net so Noah shut off the motor and soon we were pulling the trap up to the boat.

"We'll empty these traps and then I think Dad will let us take the boat and look for a place for our blind," Noah said as we started working with the fish.

"I've got an idea of the kind of place you were talking about," I said.

"Good, we'll look there first."

As we were just finishing the last of the six nets in the string, Noah stopped and listened. Soon we heard the sound of an outboard coming up the channel. "Crap, I hope that's not those Gianolli boys," he said.

"You mean they come down on this part of the river? I thought they fished on the other end of town?"

"Yeah, they come down in our part of the river now and then and I don't trust them," Noah said. "I saw them a few days ago in their boat down here. I think their father is ok but that older kid of his is a kind of a mutt. He's on the football team and he and I have had issues. He's got a real bad attitude and I think he'd mess with someone else's nets without any worry. I really don't want them seeing us here."

"What do you mean issues?" I said grinning.

Noah smirked. "I knocked him on his butt a few times at practice and he took issue with it. He came at me and was threatening to re-arrange my face but I discouraged him."

I shook my head.

Just as he said it, a flat bottom boat with two kids came around the corner and started up the cut toward us. Sure enough it was Marco and Julio Gianolli, and they were very interested in what was going on. Marco, the older brother was 18 and was driving the boat. He was tall and chunky with dark curly hair worn long over his ears. He had a large Roman nose and dark eyes and a nasty scowl on his face. The younger brother Julio was also dark but not as heavy set and about 15. He was a smaller, nicer version of his brother and seemed to be more social than his older brother who was a bully and didn't mind showing it. They slowed down and stopped alongside Noah and me. Katy barked at them.

"Shut your fat dog up," Marco said.

"For one thing, she's not my dog and for another she's not that fat. She's just big boned. She's got as much right to be on this river as you do, so why don't you get the hell out of here and she'll shut up. She's only barking because she sees some garbage floating on the river," Noah said.

"Oh yeah, you're a laugh a minute Pedersen. What's that other thing in that boat, a rat?"

Karen looked up over the gunwale and growled. "Why don't you two go and run your boat someplace else, this is a big river. Go stink it up somewhere else."

Julio, the younger brother looked embarrassed. "Come on Marco, let's go. We don't have any business here."

March scowled at his little brother. "We got as much right to this spot as they do. Why don't you guys leave?"

Noah picked up a small carp and threw it across the open water and hit Marco right in the head. "Here, go chew on this," he said. I broke out laughing and Katy barked.

Marco wiped the fish slime off the side of his head and gave us a look that would kill if looks could kill.

"You wait Pedersen, you too Larsen, one of these days we'll see who's so smart." Marco pulled the starter cord on the outboard and they roared off, throwing a wake of water up against the side of Noah's boat.

"Those dopes...dang I hate it that they saw our fish traps. It'd be just like those idiots to steal our fish. They have no ethics at all."

"I doubt they'd bother them. Your dad would go and kill them."

"Yeah, I doubt they'd have the balls to do anything."

We finished up with the last net and re-set it and then headed back down the channel and back toward home. When we got to the dock we tied up and unloaded the fish. Once they were hauled to the fish shack Noah asked his dad if we could use the boat for our duck blind scouting.

"Sure, but you better check the oil and fill it with gas," his dad said. We did as told and then Noah ran up to the fish market and grabbed a slab of smoked fish, a chunk of cheese and some soda crackers. He brought a jug of cold water and we got the dogs and headed out on the river.

We went out to the main channel and began to work our way upriver looking for a backwater lake that was close to the channel. I wanted to look at a particular place I thought would be what we were looking for, so I guided Noah and we went there.

Noah smiled when he saw where I was taking him. There was a long thin island, maybe three quarters of a mile long and it bordered the channel on one side and a huge cattail and lily pad lake on the other. About half way down the length of the island there was a break where a channel had cut back into the lake.

"Slow down," I said as we approached the cut. Noah slowed the boat to an idle.

"See here? If we build our blind right at this cut in the island, we could hunt puddle ducks like mallards and wood ducks on the pond side and later when the diving ducks come down, we could hunt the channel on the other side."

"And the island has enough trees that we can pull the boat up on it down there a little way and it won't be noticed by the ducks."

"Wow, you're right this is perfect," Noah said. "We can build our blind right on the tip of the lower part of the cut."

"Yeah, that's what I was thinking," I said.

"Good deal, this is the spot."

We grinned at each other and pulled up on the island and ate our lunch and shared it with the dogs. Then we started back down the river. We were confident that our duck blind was going to be in a place that would guarantee lots of great shooting in the coming weeks.

CHAPTER 4

WHEN WE GOT BACK to the landing we went up to the fish house. Steffen, and Jorgen were just finishing up cleaning the fish from the fish traps.

"Sure, you get here when all the work is done," his grandpa said laughing.

"We hauled them from the river, doesn't that count for work?" Noah asked.

"That's the fun part," Jorgen said. "Ripping the guts out of them isn't as much fun as riding around in the boat."

"Well, I guess you're right about that," Noah said.

"You and Sebastian can go and haul some ice up and ice the fish down if you'd like to help us," his grandpa said.

"Sure, glad to," Noah said and we went down to the market and filled a large cart with ice chips from the ice machine. We pushed it up the walkway to the fish house and shoveled chips over the wooden boxes filled with gutted fish.

"Where are these going?" I asked.

"I'm taking them to Minneapolis on Monday morning," Steffen said.

Once the fish were iced down, we loaded the boxes into the cooler and then cleaned up the fish house and shut off the lights. As we walked up to the market Noah said, "So we can tear down the little smoker?"

"Yeah, we have no use for it now," his grandpa said. "Take what wood you want to use and pile the rest up and burn it."

We acknowledged that we understood and started down to the riverbank to take a look at the old smoker. It had been used for many years to smoke carp and catfish for sale in the market. It was about the size of a 'three-hole-outhouse' as his dad used to say. The smell of apple wood smoke still hung heavily in the air around the old shack. "I was thinking we'd try to take one of the ends off in one piece for a floor," Noah said. "Then we can build it up from there."

I nodded. "We might as well build it plenty big and sturdy. If we do a good job we can use if for many years."

"Yeah, I want to build it strong and tight, so if it does get cold, we won't freeze in it."

"Good idea, we've got plenty of wood."

We went to the market and got a tool box and began taking the old smoker apart. Noah got a ladder and we got on the roof and pulled the corrugated tin off. There were several pieces of it that came off intact. "We should figure out a way to have a roof on the blind that we could open for shooting and then close up if the weather gets bad. That way we could shut it up to keep dry and also shut it up to lock it so those Gianolli kids don't get into it."

"That's a good idea, I like the part about not getting wet," I said.

It was late afternoon and we had the smoker about half demolished. The first end came off so easily that we decided to take off the other end also and keep it in one piece like the first. "Let's call it a day," I said as I wiped my hands on an old rag. "Gram is making a roast for supper and I don't want to be late."

"I wouldn't be either, she makes a mean roast," Noah said.

"Why don't you come and eat with us? Dad is over on Lake Michigan working and Mom and Gram and I will be the only ones that are eating. I'm sure there'll be enough for you too."

"You don't think she'd care?"

I shrugged. "You know Gram, she'll gripe and complain but it's all just hot air."

We put the tools away and called the dogs who were snooping around the riverbank. "Why don't you bring some clothes and sleep over? We can get a good game of Canasta going after supper."

"Hey that sounds good, tomorrow's Sunday so we can go to church and then go fishing afterward."

24

Noah told his parents of our plans and they were fine with it so Noah and I and the two dogs walked up the road to Noah's house so he could get some extra clothes and his toothbrush. Then we went to my house where the smell of a pot roast filled the air.

"Oh man, smell that," Noah said as we walked in the kitchen door.

"You guys look hungry," my mother said.

"I asked Noah to come for supper and them maybe tonight we can play some cards," I said.

Grandma looked stern and then grinned. "Gunhild and I can take you young whippersnappers in cards with one hand tied behind our backs."

We grinned and went upstairs and each took a bath and put on clean clothes. When we came downstairs half an hour later the table was filled with food.

"Oh boy," Noah said.

"Sit, it's all ready," Gram said. We all held hands and I said Grace and then we dug into the food. Katy and Karen had been sleeping side by side on the floor but they both sat at attention next to the table waiting for tidbits snuck to them by Noah and me.

When supper was over and cleaned up we moved to the living room and played cards until nearly midnight.

Once during the game Gram clearly cheated and both Noah and I saw it but I shook my head no carefully. He understood not to say anything or we'd have been arguing the rest of the night. The ladies thoroughly cleaned our clocks in cards and we retired up to my bedroom with our tails between our legs.

"Your Gram cheats," Noah said.

"I know she cheats, but I'm sure not going to say anything to her. If you're brave enough, go ahead." We laughed and got undressed and got into bed in our underwear. Katy jumped up and lay down between us and Karen began to whine from the floor next to the bed.

"What's wrong Karen? Can't you get up?" I said looking over the side of the bed. The little dog wagged her tail as I reached down and lifted her up and put her between us and next to Katy. I turned out the lamp and the light from the moon and stars filled the room.

"You know what?" Noah asked.

"No...what?"

"I'm sure glad we're friends."

I smiled and looked over at my best friend. "Why's that?"

"Oh 'cause... we get along so well and our families are good friends and I don't know it's just good to have people like that in your life."

I grinned. "I wouldn't have it any other way."

Noah winked. "Me too pal. Goodnight."

Two tired boys and two tired dogs were soon asleep.

CHAPTER 5

SUNDAY MORNING DAWNED bright and sunny as the dogs began to fidget around, waking me up. I could feel a slight breeze on my face and when I opened my eyes Katy was lying with her nose within inches of my face, looking at me. "Good morning Kate," I said. The dog's tail began hammering the bed.

"Kate, be still, I have to get more beauty sleep," Noah said sleepily from the other side of the bed.

"No amount of sleep will make you beautiful," I said laughing.

Noah rolled over on his back and Karen climbed up on his chest and licked his face. "Whoa, good morning little sweetie," he said as he hugged the dog. He looked over at me. "I don't suppose we would be able to sneak out and go fishing and miss church would we?"

I shrugged. "Give it a try if you like, but I'm not taking a chance on making Gram mad at me."

Noah nodded, 'Yeah, you're right, an hour of praying isn't as bad as having Gram on your back all week."

We got up and I went in the bathroom as Noah took the dogs downstairs so they could go outside. I could hear Noah and my grandmother talking as I came out of the bathroom and dressed. Soon Noah came up the stairs, still in his underwear, eating a cinnamon roll. "I had to do some quick sleight-of-hand to get this," he said stuffing the last of the roll into his mouth. He went in the bathroom and I went downstairs where Mom and Grandma were getting breakfast ready.

"So, you two are planning on attending church with us I expect," Gram said.

"Sure Gram, we wouldn't think of anything else."

My mom looked at me and grinned. Soon Noah joined us and we sat down to eat. Just then we heard Katy and Karen barking at the door, so Noah jumped up and let them in. They sat and begged their breakfast.

After church we got our fishing poles and some bait and Noah asked his dad if we could use the little boat for the day. In addition to the big 20 foot boat they also had a 12 foot john boat with a 7hp Evinrude motor on it. It took a lot less gas to run and was fine for fishing. We loaded up the dogs and poles and headed out onto the river.

As we motored through the back cuts toward the channel we kept an eye out for more places that might be good for the duck blind. "You know, I still think that island out by the channel is the best spot," I said. "It'll be perfect when the late ducks come down."

Noah nodded. "Let's go out there and look it over."

We maneuvered through the cuts, and took a wrong turn and ended up in a slough that was only about a foot deep. After several minutes of pushing with an oar and a little cussing, we got into deeper water and came to the channel about half a mile up river from the blind site. As we motored down the river they saw the Gianolli boys going upriver out in the channel. Julio waved to us but Marco just stuck up his finger. "Nice guy," I said grinning.

"What a mutt," Noah said.

When we came to the island we pulled the boat up on the lower side of the cut that led into the backwaters and got out. The island was about twenty yards wide and covered with trees and brush. Right at the upper end there was a huge soft maple that stood on the bank. "Jeez that tree is enormous," Noah said.

"It's getting pretty close to the river. The next high water or big wind storm and it'll tip over," I said. Indeed the tree was about a third of the way out of the ground already due to waves eating the end of the island away. Big thick roots hung out into open air where there had been land some time ago.

"Yeah, that thing is going over any time." We looked at it a while and then Noah said, "Maybe we better forget about this as a blind site. If we build our blind here and that tree falls on it,

28

we're done for."

"You're right we better look for someplace else. Dang, I think this would have been a prefect spot."

We were a little disappointed but it was better to be safe than sorry. We went down a couple of back cuts and came to a favorite fishing spot. I tied the boat to an overhanging tree and we each floated a couple of hooks with small minnows on them, suspended under bobbers, down to the next treetop which was hanging into the water. In no time we started catching crappies. The dogs lay down in the bottom of the boat and slept while we boys caught a mess of crappies for supper. When we ran out of bait we pulled up our stringer and headed home.

When we got back, we took the fish to the fish cleaning shack and cleaned them up. Then we took them up to Noah's house and his mother suggested we get my mom and grandma and have a fish fry. We spent the evening together enjoying each other's company and feasting on fresh crappies.

"When will Marius be home?" Steffen asked mom.

"He called the other day and since they have such good weather yet they're scheduling extra runs from Chicago to Quebec. He figures they'll be finished early in November and then he'll be home for the winter," she said.

My dad was the engineer on a Lake Michigan ship called *Novadak*. He made real good money working there but was away from home most of the summer.

The next day was a school day and we spent the rest of the week in school so we didn't get back to dismantling the old smoker until the next weekend. We worked on it Saturday and finished up the job. We had all of the roof tin, both ends of the shack and a pile of boards and two by fours stacked up for the blind. The rest of the scrap lumber we piled and lit on fire.

"Now, we better find a spot and get working on our blind. Duck season is going to be here before we know it."

Sunday came and went and that night I woke up when Katy began whining and poking me with her nose. "What's wrong

Kate?" I said sleepily. The dog lay right against me and looked uneasy. Then I heard thunder off in the distance. "Is a storm coming? Is that what you're worried about girl?" Kate whined and I turned and put my arm around her. "You're safe, just go back to sleep."

When she was a little pup, Katy was never bothered by storms. Then one summer day a storm blew up and she was lying on the kitchen floor sleeping when a gust of wind blew in through an open window and tipped an empty pail off the sink. The pail hit Kate on the head and scared her half to death. A couple of days later another storm began to rumble in the west and Kate got up from the kitchen floor and went into the living room and lay down. I suppose she thought the kitchen wasn't safe so she'd go someplace else. Sure enough, a gust came through the living room window and blew a lamp over and it too hit her. After that whenever a storm began to grumble in the west, Kate got nervous.

The storm got closer and closer and soon rain began to beat hard against my bedroom window. I got up to close the window and looked out to see the trees whipping back and forth as the storm raged. Kate was panting and very unsettled. "It's ok Kate it's not going to hurt you."

I lay awake consoling Katy and watched as the lightning flashed, the rain pounded and the wind gusted. After ten minutes it seemed to be lessening so I closed my eyes and the next thing I knew light was shining into the bedroom. Katy was lying looking at me with her tail wagging. "Feeling a little better today?" I said as I ruffled the dog's ears.

I got up and looked out the window. "Wow there's a lot of branches and stuff in the yard. That was a big storm."

I washed up and got ready for school. Then Katy and I went downstairs for breakfast.

CHAPTER 6

"QUITE A STORM LAST NIGHT EH?" Noah said as he walked up to my locker in the hall of the school.

"No kidding, Kate was scared. I had a hot panting dog snuggled up to me for about an hour. I wonder if that big tree fell over on the island out by the river channel?"

"We should go look after school. We really need to get busy with our blind. The duck season is coming sooner than we think."

We went to our classes and after school we changed into river clothes and took the little boat out to check out a few places that we'd considered for the blind. As we came around the end of the island Noah pulled up. "Wow, look at that, the big maple did tip over, it's in the water in the channel."

We drove the boat up to the cut in the channel and sure enough the big maple had toppled over. The top of it was lying in the water clogging up half of the channel. About half of the roots of the tree were still embedded in the island and were holding it tightly in place. The other half of the roots were standing up in the air, all torn and broken but the trunk was still firmly attached to the land. We looked it over and both seemed to have the same idea.

"That might be a perfect place for the blind," I said. "Look at how big and flat that trunk is. If it's stable we could build the blind right on top of the tree trunk."

"I was thinking the same thing. We'd be up in the air a little way and wouldn't have to worry about high water flooding the blind. It sure would be solid."

We grinned at each other as we pulled the boat up on the island. The dogs jumped out and began to explore while we walked to the end of the island and looked over the downed tree. There was a big hole in the bank where the roots had been but about half of them were still firmly attached to the land. Noah stepped up to the hole and the bank broke away and he yelled as he slid down into the hole that was half filled with water. "Holy crap!" He looked up at me and I was laughing so hard I could hardly stand up.

"Oh man that was funny! One second you were right next to me and the next you just disappeared."

"I'm glad you enjoyed it so much give me a hand up out of here."

I knelt down and Noah took my hand and I pulled him out of the hole. He was solid mud from the waist down.

"Well, we're going to have to do a little bridge building if this turns out to be our blind," he said.

We climbed up on the trunk and it was as solid as a rock. The branches on the lower side of the tree had embedded themselves in the river bottom. The tree didn't move an inch as we walked around on it. "Wow, this is perfect," Noah said.

"We can trim off those upper roots so it's easy to get up here, then trim off a few branches on top and build right here on top. If we make a little bridge from the bank to the tree so we don't have to go down in that pit that the roots made it'll be perfect," I said.

"We definitely need a bridge," Noah said grinning. Then we hopped across back to the island. Noah took off his muddy shoes and pulled off his pants and walked over to the clear river water and washed them off. Then he waded in and cleaned off the mud from his legs and feet. I helped him wring out the water from his pants and he hung them over a branch to dry. "Well, let's sit and relax a while and then we can go back and get some of our lumber and begin. We sat on the river bank and talked about ideas for the blind. Once in a while the dogs came galloping back to see what we were doing and then they'd race off again down the island. Noah checked his pants and they were dry enough to put back on.

We were both grinning from ear to ear as we got into the boat.

"Oh man I'm really excited now. I thought we'd have to drive posts in the mud and all of that work but this will be a piece of cake," Noah said. I agreed.

After talking with Steffen about our plan we decided to haul our lumber out to the island after school the next day and then we'd begin working after school and on the upcoming weekend. We loaded all the lumber easily in the big boat, hauled it to the island and unloaded it the next day.

The following day Steffen had planned on setting a new string of traps so we helped him to get the job done faster. We loaded six hoop nets in the boat and took off down river to a new area that Steffen had fished the previous fall. When we got to the area Noah moved to the bow of the boat with a long pole which was marked with white markings every foot. Steffen ran along the bank until he got to an area he thought was about where he'd fished before and slowed the motor to an idle. "Check the depth," he said.

Noah pushed the pole down into the water and it went down to sixteen feet. "Sixteen, Dad," he said.

"Good Sebastian drop that block will you?"

I dropped a cement block tied to a long rope over the side and Steffen let us slide back in the current until we came to the end of the rope. "Tie a net on," he said.

Noah tied a hoop net to the rope and he and I slowly fed the net over the side until we got to the end. Then we tied another smaller block to the end and let it back until we reached the end of that rope, dropped the block and one net was set.

Steffen moved back up to the place we'd dropped the first block and Noah reached out and grabbed a small branch and tied a little piece of blue cloth to it. Then we moved down river about a hundred yards and repeated the process until we had all six nets out.

"I'm going to put out some setlines later in the week," Steffen said. "I've got a big order for catfish so I need to get a lot of equipment on the bottom of the river."

"We'll go along and help," Noah said.

"I'd sure appreciate it," his dad said.

On the way back Noah said to his father, "Hey Dad, take a left up at that island and we'll show you where we're going to build the blind. Steffen did as he instructed and soon we pulled into the cut where the tree was lying in the water. "We're going to build a little bridge from the shore to the trunk of the tree and then build the blind right on the trunk of the tree," Noah said.

His dad grinned. "That's a darn good idea. It'll be solid as heck and get you up above the high water if it comes. You'll be a little higher than if you were in the marsh too. A few feet closer to the ducks will probably help your shooting."

We were pretty happy with the approval of Steffen of our building site. On the way back to the fish market we had big smiles on our faces. We both loved the river and time spent on it was some of our best times.

The next day we helped get bait ready for the setlines. Noah and I went to an area that we used for digging worms. Our families both saved vegetable scraps and yard waste and dug it into a spot where the dirt was good and rich and lots of earthworms lived. We could dig a good bunch of worms with very little effort any day as long as there was rain occasionally, and the vegetable matter held moisture so the place never dried out really badly.

While we dug worms Noah's dad and granddad prepared cut bait. They took unwanted fish that had been saved for the last few days from the nets and cut them into small chunks. They also cut up some clams that Noah's grandpa had harvested. All of the bait was put into the cooler for the night.

The next day after school Noah and I and Steffen headed out with the set lines. We made the dogs stay home. Each setline was three hundred feet long and had fifty hooks set six feet apart on it. It was not a good idea to have two dogs in the boat with all the fish hooks involved in this type of fishing.

Steffen had loaded twelve long willow poles in the boat and

we tied one end of the first setline on one of the willows. When we got to the place Steffen wanted to fish Noah went to the front of the boat and shoved the willow into the mud.   Then Steffen moved us back away from it for about twenty feet until we came to the first hook on the line.   Noah and I sat on fish boxes and took turns baiting hooks as Steffen backed us away from the pole. We'd put a worm on one, then a piece of cut bait on the next and a piece of clam on the next. When we came to the end of the line we tied it to another pole and shoved it into the mud.

"There, one down, five to go," Steffen said.

We motored to the next spot and repeated the process and in a couple of hours we had all three hundred hooks baited and set. "Now we'll see what comes to us tonight," Steffen said as we motored back to shore.

When we got back we dug more worms, cut more bait and got everything ready for the next day. Then I went home for supper and a good night's sleep.

CHAPTER 7

WHEN I ARRIVED at the fish market Noah was talking to his dad. As I walked up I heard Noah say, "We'll go check them Dad, you go ahead and deliver the fish. Sebastian and I know what to do."

Noah turned to me. "Dad has to go to La Crosse with a load of fish so I told him we'd pull the nets and check the trotlines."

"No problem," I said. I actually enjoyed helping with the fishing. Even though it was much different than regular fishing, it was very exciting to lift a hoop net or a trotline and find what was there.

We loaded up bait for the lines and Noah cranked up the motor on the big boat. We left the dogs behind as we had before because of the hundreds of fishhooks that would be in the boat. It was not good to think of Katy or Karen scampering around with hooks and lines all over the place. Of course we got that "What are you doing leaving us behind!" look from them as we motored away. Karen actually jumped off the dock and began swimming after us but thought better of it after a while and turned back.

We motored to the nets that we'd set out and pulled up to the first marker. I hooked the rope and we lifted the net and began working to the back end of it. When the end came up we saw that the net was empty. "Holy cow, not a thing," Noah said shaking his head.

"Does that happen very often?" I asked.

"No, not often at all, there's usually a few fish in a net after this long. This is a new area too. There should be a lot of fish here."

We lowered the net and moved up to the next set and it was the same thing. Not a fish. Noah got a frown on his face. "Something's funny here and I don't mean funny ha ha."

By the time we got to the last net Noah was convinced of his suspicion. "Somebody got to these and emptied them before we got here. There's no way all six nets would be empty, absolutely no way."

"Who would do it?"

"If I had to guess I'd be guessing Gianolli. Those two were pretty interested in where we were setting. They might have stumbled onto our markers or have been hiding and watching us set."

"You really think they'd do that?"

"I wouldn't put it past Marco. I don't think Julio is a bad kid but he's with that stupid Marco he doesn't have much choice does he? Well, let's go check the trotlines and hope we have better luck on them."

We motored to the bay where we'd set the trotlines and Noah took us to the end of one of the lines. I grabbed the willow pole and held onto it and Noah shut off the engine and moved some fish boxes into position. Then he sat down on a couple of overturned boxes and got the bait pails ready. "Ok, you pull us along the line and I'll take off the fish and re-bait."

I took a stick with a hook on the end and hooked the line and began pulling the boat down the line. An empty hook came up first and as it got to Noah he put a piece of clam on it and let it go past. The next hook was also empty and he put a chunk of cut up shiner on that one. There was a nice fat catfish on the third hook so Noah took it off and tossed it into a fish box and then baited the hook with a fat night crawler.

We worked our way across the line finding a fish on every third or fourth hook. By the time we got across the whole line we had a good start on filling up the boxes. "I'll stay here, you start her up and take us up to the next line," Noah said to me.

I started the motor and steered us to the next willow pole. I shut off the motor and walked quickly to the front of the boat and grabbed the pole, hooked the line and began working us across the bay. This line produced about the same amount of fish. "It's a good thing we set these out. Dad would be unhappy if he got back and found we didn't have any fish to sell," Noah said.

We were checking the fourth of the lines when we heard the sound of an outboard motor coming up from behind the island. In a minute the Gianolli boys came around the end of the island and saw us. "Oh great, now they've seen our trotlines too," Noah said.

Marco Gianolli steered toward us and cut the motor as he got a short distance away. "Havin' any luck Pederson?"

"None of your business Gianolli. What are you guys doing down in this part of the river. I thought you fished the upper stretch."

"Whadda ya think you own the river? We can fish anywhere we like."

"That's true Gianolli, but if you mess with another fisherman's lines or nets you'll go to jail."

"You accusing us of stealing your fish?"

"I'm not accusing you of anything but if we find out you're messing with our gear, we'll have the Game Warden on your ugly butt quicker than you think."

The younger brother was sitting in the bow of the boat and looked worried but said nothing.

"Don't worry Pederson you won't catch us doing anything."

With that Marco started the motor and gunned it. His boat shot forward and narrowly missed hitting Noah's boat. I lost my balance and fell forward. The wake from Gianolli's boat hit the side of Noah's boat and when it did the boat lurched to the side. I fell and my hand slid down the line to the next hook. The wave lifted the boat and the hook sunk into the palm of my hand. It felt like a knife had been plunged into my palm and I let out a scream of pain. The boat rocked again in the wave and the next thing I knew I was being dragged over the side into the water.

"Holy smokes!" Noah said just as I went under the water.

He jumped up and ran to the front of the boat. He couldn't see me because the tension of the line had pulled me to the bottom along with the other hooks. "He's hooked and it drug him over!"

he yelled to Gianolli.

Marco sat looking kind of stupid but Julio pulled off his shoes and stood up and dove over the side of their boat into the water. Noah did the same and soon the two of them were underwater looking for me. Of course I didn't know this at the time but Noah told me afterward.

I had gotten a good breath as I went over the side but my lungs were beginning to burn as I tried to get to the surface. The line was tight between the poles and some of the hooks still had fish on them so it was nearly impossible for me to get up. I knew Noah would be in the water looking for me so I tried to stay calm and not use up my oxygen.

Meanwhile Noah was on the bottom sweeping his arms back and forth trying to locate the line. The water was too murky for him to see anything. When he found the line he swam for the surface. I could feel myself being pulled up with the line. When Noah got to the top of the water Julio had just come up for a breath. "I've got the line," he yelled. Julio swam to him and helped him pull up on the line. They worked on it until they saw my free hand coming up out of the water. Julio grabbed my hand and pulled me up.

I came to the top coughing and gasping for breath. "My hand, it's hooked."

While Julio held my head above water Noah reached into his pocket and pulled out his jack knife. He opened the blade and then cut the line he was holding onto. I was able to raise my hooked hand up and Noah cut the line on the other side and I was free. They began to help me toward the big boat which had now drifted away.

"Get over here and help us!" Julio yelled to his brother.

Marco cranked up the motor and pulled up to us. Between Noah and Julio they managed to get me up and into the boat. Then Julio climbed in and Noah swam to the big boat and climbed over the stern. Marco moved his boat next to Noah's and they helped me across.

Noah looked at my hand. The hook was in very deeply and right in the fat part of my palm next to my thumb. "Ouch, we better get you back and let Gram look at that," he said.

I was shaking and nodded in agreement. I felt sick to my stomach looking at the hook embedded in my hand and I was cold from being on the bottom for what seemed like a very long time. I began to shake and shiver.

Noah started the engine and looked over at Julio. "Thanks, I don't think I could have gotten him alone."

Julio nodded and grinned. "Maybe you can do the same for me some day."

"Thanks Julio," I said.

Marco just sat there and never said a word.

We took off down the river as fast as the big boat would go.

CHAPTER 8

THE BLEEDING HAD NEARLY STOPPED by the time we got back to the boat landing at the fish market. There was just a little blood oozing out around the hook. Noah nudged the boat up to the dock and tied it up as I waited for a hand up onto the wooden platform. "How's it feeling?" Noah asked.

"Right now it's just a dull ache," I said. "At first it felt like a knife was slicing into me. But I was more worried about drowning as I sunk to the bottom of the river."

"I'm glad Julio was there to help," Noah said as we walked up the road. "I don't know if I'd have been able to get you up alone."

We didn't go into the fish market because Noah's dad and grandpa were gone delivering the fish and their hired man was tending the store. It was only a short walk to my house anyway. When we got there we stopped on the porch and Noah helped me get my shoes off after he had his own off. Together we walked in our wet socked feet into the kitchen where Gram was stirring something on the stove.

"Well, there they are," Gram said. "How was fishing today?"

"Not good Gram, someone stole our fish from the traps and we had a little accident with the trotlines."

Gram turned and looked shocked when she was my bloody hand. "What in the world?"

"We had some trouble and I got a hook in my hand," I said holding the injured hand out.

"Sit at the table," Gram said and went to the bathroom to fetch her First Aid kit. Soon she returned and began working on my hand. I grimaced as she prodded the hook. Noah turned his head not wanting to look.

"It's past the barb pretty far," the old lady said. "I think we're going to have to push it through and cut the barb off."

I swallowed hard. "You can't just back it up?"

"I'll try but I'm afraid it won't come out that way."

Gram got a bowl of warm water and a wash cloth and cleaned the area around the hook. Then she took hold of the shank of the hook and pulled gently. I gasped as the hook moved. "Oh man," I whispered. My ears started to ring and I felt a little dizzy.

Noah took a quick glance and then turned his head away again.

"It's not going to come that way," Gram said. "I'm going to have to push it until it comes through. Then I'll take a wire cutter and cut the barb off. It's the only way."

I nodded. "Go ahead if that's what we have to do, let's get it over with."

Gram pulled a pair of pliers out of her kit and grabbed the shank again. "Ok, here we go," she said. She pushed the hook and the flesh on my hand puckered up as the point of the hook pushed upward. I shut my eyes and gritted my teeth. She pushed a little harder and the point of the hook could be seen just under the skin. "Almost there," she said.

My ears began ringing and I felt like I was going to pass out. "Hold it a minute Gram!" I said gasping. "Let me rest a minute."

Gram backed off and wiped my forehead with the towel.

"Just tell me when you're ready," she said.

Noah turned his head and took a peek at the hand and then turned away again quickly. I nodded for Gram to begin again and she pushed again and suddenly there was a crash. Gram and I turned and looked as Noah tipped over and fell to the floor under the table. "Holy smokes!" I said.

"Just leave him be, I'll take care of him once we get this finished."

Gram pushed again and the point of the hook broke through the skin. My forehead was dripping in sweat by now. Then she pushed the barb through. She took her needle nose and turned it on its side and clipped the end of the hook off, slid it backwards and in a second it was out of my hand. "Take some of that alcohol and dab it into that hole in your hand while I take a look at this big brave Viking."

I poured some rubbing alcohol onto a cotton ball and grimaced as the stinging liquid penetrated into the wound. Gram knelt beside Noah just as he began to stir. "Wha...what happened?" he said looking around dazed. '

"You fainted you big dummy," Gram said. "I thought you Danes were suppose to be descended from the Vikings," she laughed.

Noah looked up. "I've never been good with stuff like that. Once I cut my finger cleaning a fish and when I passed out I cut a bigger gash in my head when I hit the fish table."

"Well, I guess being a doctor isn't going to be for you," I said grinning.

"Nope, not even close...are you fixed?"

I held up my hand. The bleeding had stopped and there were two little holes in the palm of my hand next to my thumb. "It's going to be sore for a while but I think I'll live," I said.

Gram put some Iodine on the hand and wrapped a bandage around it. "Try to keep it clean and dry for a while," she said. "We'll watch it to be sure it doesn't get infected."

"We're going to change into some dry clothes," I said. Noah and I walked upstairs and I lent him some of my clothes to change into. They were fine except for the length of the jeans which were a little short in the legs for him. We went back downstairs just as Gram put the cookie jar on the table and sat two glasses and a bottle of milk down for us.

"So what were you talking about when you said someone took your fish?"

"All of the new hoop nets we put out the other day were empty, not one fish in any of them."

"Maybe you just put them out in the wrong place."

"No way, there'd be at least a few fish in them. The Gianolli boys saw us in that area the other day and we figure they found our markers and lifted the nets and took the fish before we got there."

"Your dad isn't going to like that," Gram said.

"I'm not sure I should tell him," Noah said. "He'll go up there and might get himself into trouble with Mr. Gianolli if he knows what happened."

"Well he should shouldn't he?"

"No I don't think it was Mr. Gianolli, it was that bonehead of a son of his, the older one Marco. He thinks he can do anything he wants. I wouldn't put it past him to mess with another fisherman's nets at all."

"Well, you two better think of something to do to make him stop or your dad will find out and then things will get out of hand."

Noah looked at me. "You're right Gram, we'll think of something. You just keep this to yourself ok?"

"Not a word," the old lady said making a zipping motion across her lips.

I grinned at Noah. "So what you got in mind?"

CHAPTER 9

NOAH AND I WALKED back to the fish market and while we walked we tried to think of a way to get the Gianolli boys to leave the fish traps alone. "We've got to do something that makes it impossible for him to deny he was the one who stole our fish," Noah said.

"How are we going to do that? It's his word against ours."

"Maybe not, if we make it impossible for him to deny it," he said.

I grinned at him. "You've got that evil look in your eyes."

Noah nodded. "I've got an idea but first we've got to go and finish pulling those trotlines so we've got some fish for Dad to sell. If we do that he may not even think about the fish traps."

My hand was still hurting but I thought I could stand it to help. "Get me one of those heavy rubber gloves and I'll come and help," I said.

A half hour later we were back at the trotlines working our way across the river pulling up the hooks. It took us nearly two hours to check and bait all the hooks but when we were finished we had a good load of fish with many of them being catfish.

"Dad'll be happy with these," Noah said.

We took the fish in, loaded them onto the carts and hauled them up to the cleaning house. After the fish were cleaned and iced Noah and I walked into town. We stopped at the hardware store.

"You got any money?" he asked.

"I've got a couple of dollars," I said.

"I think that'll be enough with what I've got," he said.

"What are we buying?"

"Paint."

We were lucky and found a gallon of paint that had been mixed wrong and was off-color. A farmer had wanted a deep red for his barn and somehow the paint had come out pink. We got the gallon for a dollar and headed back to the fish market.

"I'm going to get some rope and a few things, I'll meet you in the boat," Noah said.

A few minutes later Noah came walking down the boat dock with a roll of rope, two halves of a cement block and a ball of string. He was grinning like mad as he started up the big motor on the boat and headed us out to the river.

We went to the new string of hoop nets and Noah idled along until he found what he was looking for. He pulled the boat into the shore on the island next to the hoop nets and looked up into a big maple tree that stood next to the river.

"Are we going squirrel hunting?" I asked laughing.

"Nope, we're going skunk hunting."

I watched as Noah tied the gallon of paint onto the rope and then hopped out onto the bank. He walked to the big maple and began to climb up into the branches. After a few minutes he was out on a branch that hung out over the river. He'd tied the rope to the belt loop of his jeans. He pulled the rope up into the tree and the bucket of paint went up with it. Then he measured a length of rope and tied the rope around the big branch he was sitting on. Then he moved back on the branch. As he moved back toward the trunk of the tree he pulled the can of paint up into the tree with him. I couldn't tell exactly what he was doing up in the tree but eventually I could see that the paint was hanging from the branch next to the trunk of the tree. The rope that the paint was hanging on was tied with a piece of the string he'd brought out near the end of the branch so the paint was hanging by the string but still attached to the rope.

Noah reached into his pocket and took his jack knife out and pried the lid off the paint but sat the lid back on top of the can loosely. Then he tied another piece of the rope to the handle of the can and jumped down from the tree. He concealed the rope in the leaves and brush. Then he came and got the other piece of cement block and laid it at the bottom of the tree. He fed the rope from the paint can through the hole in the block and worked his way to the riverbank and tossed the loose end across to me in the boat. "Hold onto this until I get over there."

I was grinning because now I knew what he had in mind.

Noah got back into the boat and started the motor. "Get that cement block ready and tie it to that rope," he said. I did as he instructed and he carefully moved the boat out away from the bank while I played out the line. When it was about tight I dropped the block to the bottom of the river. Noah then pulled a little strip of cloth from his pocket and handed it to me. "Tie it on and be sure it's easy to see," he said.

I stood on the bow of the boat and tied the cloth to a branch and we backed away. Noah sat and looked onto the island carefully. "If you look real close you can see that rope but I don't think the Gianolli boys will be looking for a trap. Once they see the cloth they'll hook the rope and begin pulling it up. When it gets tight it'll break that string holding up the paint and the can will swing out and hopefully will hit one of them and cover them with pink paint.

I couldn't help but laugh. "Jeez, you're a devious devil."

Noah just grinned.

We headed back to the fish market and home for the day.

With any luck the trap would work and the Gianolli boys would leave our fish alone from now on, and Noah's dad wouldn't ever have to know. At least that was the plan.

Chapter 10

"**We're going to have** to keep Dad from that string of hoop nets for the next few days so he doesn't get caught in our trap," Noah said the next morning at school. "I said something to him this morning about you and me checking them for him since we had set them and he said that was fine with him. He's got a lot of fish to smoke for a big order that he has to deliver this weekend, so we have to hope our fish thieves will get caught by then."

We were standing next to my locker talking about the trap when Marco Gianolli came strolling down the hallway. He gave us a dirty look and walked on past. Julio was a little way behind him and nodded to us and smiled a bit. "Sorry about my brother," he said.

"No problem Julio, you can't choose your relatives," I said.

After school Noah and I took the big boat out and checked all three of the strings of hoop nets. There were good numbers of fish in the first two older strings so we were nearly loaded down with fish when we finished with them. We took the full fish boxes back to the landing and unloaded them and then went downriver to the new string. This time there were some fish in each of the nets. When we got to the booby trapped set we carefully gave it wide berth.

"Don't you think they'll notice the rope coming from the shore?" I said.

"No, I ran it under a low branch so it'll be real low in the water. They only have to pull it a little way and that string will break and the paint will come swinging out on the rope. They won't know what hit them."

We were both grinning as we rode up the river and back to the dock.

The next day at school we made a big deal about telling it around that we were going to start on our duck blind that night and wouldn't be checking our hoop nets. Noah also let it be known that his dad was out of town. We knew that Marco would think he had open season on our nets and hoped he'd try for them.

After school we loaded up a bunch of lumber and one of the ends of the old smoker and took them out to the island near the channel. Katy and Karen went with us and took off, to look around while Noah and I unloaded the lumber on the island. We had a saw with us and carefully skirted around the hole where the roots had been and climbed up on the tree. We began sawing off roots and branches that were going to be in the way of the blind. It was hard work because many of the branches were as thick as your leg and took a lot of sawing. When we got done we were both pretty well tired out.

We called the dogs and headed back toward the dock. "Let's swing down that channel with the new hoop nets and just see if things have been messed with," Noah said as we cruised down the river.

I nodded in agreement and a few minutes later we were in the channel where our trap had been set. Noah began laughing as we got near the trap. There was pink paint all over the leaves on the shoreline plants and the empty paint bucket was hanging from the rope out over the river.

"Holy crap, it worked!" I said grinning.

"No foolin'"

We pulled into shore and Noah climbed up the tree and cut the rope down. We pulled it into the boat and cut off the empty paint can. I rolled up the rope while Noah drove us back to the dock. When we got back I carefully hid the empty paint can in the trash can and Noah put the rope away.

We put our tools away and went home, with great expectations of what we'd find at school the next day.

We were standing by my locker when Julio came walking down the hallway. He was grinning and we could see a little pink paint in his hair at the back of his head. He stopped by us.

"Good one," he said.

"What do you mean?" I said trying not to laugh.

"Oh wait till you see Marco. I think this taught him a lesson."

"It worked pretty good?" Noah said.

Julio nodded. "Hey I hope you guys know that wasn't my idea to mess with your fish traps."

"We know, we knew that right away. Like we said before, you can't choose your family."

Just then there was a lot of laughter coming from down the hall and we could see other kids pointing and laughing. The crowd parted and there came Marco. He had the pinkest hair we'd ever seen and his ears face and neck looked like they'd been scrubbed with steel wool. His face was bright red, not only from embarrassment but from trying to clean all the paint from his skin. His ears and the inside of his ears were still pink as was his normally black curly hair. His clothes were clean but his shoes were pink also.

"You guys are gonna pay," he growled as he got to us.

"Pay for what Marco?" Noah asked.

"Pay for slopping paint all over me."

"Why do you think it was us that slopped paint all over you?" I asked.

"The paint was right where your hoop... um, I just know."

Noah stepped up to the bigger kid and got nose to nose with him. "Listen you bonehead, it's a crime to touch anyone's lines or nets and if you're caught doing it you lose your commercial fishing license for a year. If you want us to go to the Game Warden and explain what happened, we'll be happy to. Then you can file a complaint against us for the booby trap. But at the same time you'll be admitting that you were messing with our hoop nets. It's up to you but we're willing to let it go at this. As long as you leave our nets and lines alone we're done. If not we've got problems."

Marco stood there boiling mad but knew he'd been bested. "Just you watch out Pederson, you and Larson are in my sights."

He stomped off down the hallway.

"Thanks guys for letting it go at that," Julio said. "If our dad found out that Marco had been bothering your nets he'd have taken him out and beat the hell out of him."

"We're cool Julio," Noah said.

Julio turned and walked away and we grinned at each other. Noah got a goofy look on his face. "Oooooh, we're in Marco's sights Sebastian," he said.

"Yeah, I'm shaking in my shoes," I said.

We laughed all the way to class.

Chapter 11

WE HAD THE JOHN BOAT loaded down the next Saturday morning as we headed out to the island where our duck blind was going to be built. In addition to the two dogs we had hammers, hand saws, a couple of empty bean cans full of nails and a basket full of lunch. We also had a drill and wrench and several long lag bolts. Gram had insisted on making us enough food for a small army just in case we got hungry during our blind construction work.

When we pulled up on the island Katy and Karen took off through the brush exploring as usual while Noah and I carried the tools and nails to the end of the island.

"The bridge is the first thing we need," I said.

Noah agreed and he climbed around the root hole and got out onto the tree trunk while I held a measuring rule across. He put the end where it needed to be and I took a reading. I selected two of the old rafters from the smoker that were made from 2 x 6's and cut them off at the proper length. I slid one across and tossed a hammer to Noah and he pulled a couple of nails from his pocket and nailed the board down. Then we did the same with the second one and I dug grooves into the dirt to anchor the shore end. Noah came back across and we measured the gap between the rafters and began cutting 1 x 6 planks to nail down as the surface of the bridge. It didn't take long and we had worked our way across the gap nailing down the planks. We were both on the tree side of the gap when the dogs came galloping back to us.

"Hey Kate, can you come over here?" I said patting my leg.

Katy looked down at the bridge and then at me and stood there, not sure of what to do. Noah walked part way across the bridge and called the dogs; they both trotted across to us.

"Well, that wasn't as hard as I thought it might be," I said.

We shooed the dogs back across and then went back and picked up the end of the old smoker that we'd left in one piece. It was about 5 feet wide and 6 feet long and we planned on using it for the floor of the blind. Noah took one end and began backing across the bridge with me on the other end. It was a little scary walking across not being able to see where my feet were going but we made it and set the platform down on the tree trunk. It fit pretty well but we needed a shim here and there to make it level. Once it was all leveled and right where we wanted it we nailed it down.

Then we got the drill out and drilled holes through the floor frame into the tree trunk and limbs that were in the right places. Once we had the holes drilled I began to put 6 inch lag bolts through the floor and into the wood of the tree. This floor was not going to go anywhere.

"If it gets windy or we have high water or big waves we sure won't have to worry about the blind flying off the tree," I said as I tightened the last bolt."

"This thing will probably outlast us," Noah said surveying our work. He jumped up and down on the platform and it was as solid as concrete.

"Wow, this is going to be a huge blind," I said.

"Maybe we're overdoing it," Noah said looking at the big platform.

"Well, this way we can have room to move around and the dogs will have room. I don't see why we should make it tiny if we have all this wood."

Noah agreed and we began to measure and cut boards and in a couple of hours we had a good start on the walls of the blind. We took a break and sat on the sandy shore of the island and ate lunch and shared with the dogs. After lunch we lay back on the beach and rested for a while.

"Let's work for another hour or so and then tomorrow we can come out after church and try to finish it," I said.

Noah thought that was a good idea and we made good

progress during the next hour. We had the front wall up, the river-side wall and part of the marsh-side wall. Tomorrow we'd finish the marsh wall and work on the back wall and the door. Once we had the walls up we planned on cutting a boat full of grass and then tying it into bundles and fastening them to the outside of the blind to camouflage it. We were both tired and dirty as we motored back to the dock but we were really proud of the work we'd gotten done.

Sunday after church we went back to the island and finished up the last two walls. We made a door in the middle of the back wall so we could open it from the bridge and get inside the blind. Our plan was to put a roof over the back part of the blind so we'd stay dry and warm and also build a roof over the front that we could open when we were hunting but close up at night to keep the blind safe from anyone who might want to swipe our stuff. We had the tin from the roof and several hinges that we'd salvaged from the old smoker.

Inside we planned on building stools to sit on and a little dog door and bridge in front so Katy could see out and watch where the ducks fell when we shot them. Then she could go down the dog bridge and swim out to get them for us. At least that was the plan. We'd have to see what Katy thought about it but she loved to hunt and retrieve ducks so we figured that once she figured out how it worked she'd be happy to do it.

Karen on the other hand would probably have to just sit and watch. Her little short legs made it hard for her to get up and down the steep island and she really didn't enjoy the water as much as Katy did anyway. She liked to go along but preferred to stay dry most of the time.

"Tomorrow after school let's go to the marsh and cut some grass and begin to cover it," I said.

"Sounds good to me," Noah said as we motored home.

CHAPTER 12

WE TOOK THE SMALL BOAT the next day when we got back from school and headed out to the marsh. We left the dogs home and got a couple of terribly hurt looks from them when we pulled out away from the dock.

"Jeez I feel like a criminal when I look at those dogs. They act like we're horrible people leaving them behind," Noah said.

I laughed. "They'll forget about it once we're out of sight. We can't have them in the boat once we get it full of cattails and grass. The idea is to lay all the grass down in nice straight bundles and with two dogs climbing all over it they'd ruin most of it."

We got to the marsh and pulled the boat next to a large patch of cattails and swamp grass. We both had on hip boots and stepped out over the side of the boat into the mud and water. Noah had a machete with him and we waded into the thick grass. I gathered a large bunch of grass and held it while he hacked it loose from the roots. Then I waded back to the boat and laid the bundle of grass in the bottom and went back for another. We changed jobs after a while and in less than half an hour we had a boat full of grass.

"That's plenty for now," I said.

We climbed into the boat and headed back toward the dock. We had to go slow so the grass didn't blow out of the boat and when we got back the two dogs came running down to greet us. They were all excited over the grass and seemed to have forgotten how horrible we had been to them.

We unloaded the grass and piled it next to the fish cleaning table. "Tomorrow we can work on making a mat from it," I said.

"Man this is going to be the best blind on the river," Noah said with a big grin. I had to agree. After all of the work we were going through, we better shoot a lot of ducks from it too.

The next day after school we stopped by the hardware store and bought a roll of twine that the farmers used for bailing hay. We took it down to the fish cleaning table and pulled off a couple of pieces that were about twenty feet long. Then we doubled them over and laid them about twenty inches apart on the table. I picked up a big handful of grass and laid it on the table between the two pieces of twine. Then Noah took one and I picked up the other and we tied the twine around the bundle of grass. Then we put another bundle of grass between the double lines and tied it in. We kept working and tying in bundles until we got to the end of our twine lines. We ended up with about a 10 foot grass mat. "Wow, that's really nice," Noah said.

The bundles were tied next to each other and looked like those grass huts you saw in South Seas movies. We rolled the mat of grass up and tied a piece of twine around it.

"There, that's about ten feet of grass," I said. "Now we need to get about three times that much and we can cover the sides. If we figure out the roof we can make some more for it and our blind will look like a big pile of grass that washed up in a flood."

Noah shook his head. "Sometimes you amaze me with your ideas," he said grinning.

"An old Norse trick," I said.

We cut grass and made another mat the next day and then took the big boat the following day with some of the roof tin and some lumber to try to figure out what to do with the roof.

When we got to the blind we measured the outside and found that we needed about eight more feet of mat to finish covering it.

"What if..." Noah said looking at the roof.

"What if what?"

"I was thinking that we'd cover the back half of the roof and make it solid. Then we could put a good strong two by six across the front edge of it and make another half a roof and hinge it to the back. That way when we come to hunt, we can open the top and lay it back on the back half. We can stand and shoot from the front half. Then when we're done we can close it and even lock it from the inside and everything in the blind will be safe and dry."

I grinned. "Not bad, but what about camouflaging it?"

If we attach the mat to the inside of the front part it'll be covered with grass when we open it. We can paint the tin some brown color to hide it more when we're not here but who cares what it looks like when we're not hunting. The ducks will get used to it anyway."

"I think that's a good idea. I like the thought of locking it up. With Marco Gianolli around anything we leave out here will be gone. Ok, let's figure out how to do this."

We began measuring and I picked up a short piece of plank that we'd left behind and sketched out the plan for the roof. Once we had all of our measurements we went down to the boat and began to cut boards and tin. By the time we got the material all cut to size it was getting dark so we packed up the tools and piled the material on the shore.

As we motored back through the back channels I looked back to see a huge grin on Noah's face. "What's so funny?" I said over the sound of the motor?"

"Nothing, I was just thinking of how nice and warm we'll be in that blind compared to how we hunted the last year. I'm sure not going to miss freezing my butt off standing in the cold water."

I nodded in agreement. Little did I know how much more that blind would do besides keep us warm and dry.

CHAPTER 13

THAT NIGHT A STORM FRONT moved in and the weather went from blue skies to clouds and wind. In the morning it was raining as I walked to school. Noah was at his locker laughing with some of our friends when I got to school.

"What's so funny?" I asked.

"I was telling them why Marco had such funny looking hair a while ago. These guys were afraid to ask him for fear he'd freak out on them."

Just then Marco Gianolli came past and heard his name mentioned. He shoved his way up to Noah and stood there nose to nose with him. "What's your problem Pederson?"

Noah backed up. "Until just now I had no problem but now that you ask, your breath smells like the inside of my hip boot, so I guess that's my problem."

Marco shoved Noah back into his locker. Everyone started to push forward telling them to stop but Noah regained his balance and before we knew it his right fist came up and connected with Marco's nose scoring a direct hit. Marco's nose began to bleed like a stuck hog and a couple of our friends grabbed him as he started forward toward Noah.

"Knock it off, you're gonna get expelled for fighting," one of them said to Marco.

"He hit me first!"

"Yeah after you shoved him," I said. "I'm sure the principal will ask the rest of us who started it so shut up and let it go."

Marco looked at me. "I knew you'd stand up for your girlfriend Larson."

"Don't press your luck Marco. Let it go."

He stood there glaring at Noah and me and then stomped off toward the boy's bathroom. Noah grinned. "Your girlfriend?"

I laughed. "You'd make one ugly girlfriend old pal."

We all had a good laugh and just then the bell rang and we headed off to our classes. Every time we saw Marco the rest of the day he glared at us. Julio came past later and grinned. "Marco's nose looks a little sore, did you give him that?"

Noah nodded and Julio laughed and grinned. "No doubt he deserved it."

The nasty weather lasted for two days and finally it cleared up just in time for the weekend. Noah and I loaded up the tools into the little boat and went to the island to finish up the roof of the blind. Our plan worked just as we had expected and in about three hours we were finishing up the hinges and latch on the front roof panel. The back part of the roof was all built and ready for the tin and then the grass and paint. Once we had the front finished we decided to quit for the day and go fishing for some crappies.

"I could eat a few dozen crappie fillets," Noah said as we motored back to the dock to get our fishing poles and some bait.

"What, just a few dozen? Are you on a diet?" I said grinning.

Half an hour later, we tied the boat to an overhanging tree branch that was just above a big treetop that had toppled into the water a few months later. We each baited up a hook with a little jig and a piece of worm and floated them down in the current until they were close to the tree branches. It didn't take long until my bobber went down and I reeled in a nice big crappie. We had a fish bag over the side of the boat and in no time we had about three dozen big crappies in the bag.

"Let's go fillet these and have a fish fry," I said.

"Yeah, I'm getting pretty weak from hunger," Noah said.

We started up the cut to the channel to the boat landing and just as we came around the corner we saw Marco Gianolli turning into a channel above us.

"What's that mutt doing down here again?" Noah said.

I shook my head. "It can't be good. Why's he so angry at you? Is it just because you flattened him in football?"

"I don't know, I suppose that and the paint. He's always had a chip on his shoulder it seems. I remember back in grade school he was always messing with me when he was bigger than me. Then I got my growth spurt and now he's not so tough. It might have something to do with Angie Evans though. Marco fancied himself to be her boyfriend but Angie didn't think so. I took her to the homecoming dance last year and that really made him mad. But the poor girl, she craved her Danish god, so what could I do?"

I laughed. "It's too bad he's such a dope. I wouldn't mind getting to know Julio. He seems like a nice kid."

Noah agreed with me. We motored back to the dock and were unloading the boat when Noah's dad came walking down to the dock. "Oh great, crappies for supper," he said.

"There should be enough for both of our families," Noah said. "How about you call your mom and Gram and have them come down and we can all have a fish fry together."

"Sounds good," I said.

I looked at Steffen and he was looking out at the river curiously. "What's wrong?" I asked.

"Smoke," he said.

I turned and looked and could see way out above the islands toward the channel side of the river. There was a lot of smoke rising up from somewhere near the channel.

"Do you suppose it's a boat on fire?" I asked.

"If it was a boat it would probably be black smoke from the oil and gas. This is white smoke like its wood burning."

"It might be a barge," I said.

"It could be but it doesn't seem to be moving. I'd say it's on one of the islands close to the channel."

I looked at Noah. "You don't suppose....."

"Dad can you take these fish?" he said. "We gotta go check on our duck blind."

CHAPTER 14

"NOAH, SLOW THIS THING DOWN or you're gonna kill us!" I yelled over the noise of the outboard motor. We were flying down channels and sliding around the corners heading toward the smoke that was billowing up out near the channel.

We slid around a sharp corner of an island and nearly slammed into a row boat with an old man in it who was fishing bluegills along the edge of a lily pad bed. There was an old golden retriever with a white face sitting on the front seat of the boat and he nearly fell overboard when the wake hit the boat. The old man grabbed the sides of the boat and looked at us with a scowl.

"Sorry!" Noah said as he cut the motor back to ¾ throttle and kept on going.

I lifted my hands palm up and said, "We're sorry sir, hope you weren't hurt."

I looked at Noah and he had a determined look on his face. "Noah, if it's the blind we're going to be too late, slow down and we'll get there soon enough," I said.

He looked at me and nodded. "Yeah, I guess if it's the blind we're too late anyway."

We cut back to a sensible speed and continued toward the smoke. The closer we got the more sick I felt in my stomach. Unless the smoke was on an island on the other side of the channel opposite from our blind, it was surely the blind burning.

We came around the last island and sure enough, the blind was on fire and nearly burnt completely down. Noah slowed down and we pulled up on the island a little way away from the blind and got out. We walked up to the end of the island and just stood there looking at the smoldering wood of the floor. The roof and walls were gone and a part of the floor was still there but burnt beyond repair. The bridge was scorched on the outside end but hadn't burned much at all.

"That damn Gianolli!" Noah said shaking his head.

"We can't be sure he did it," I said.

He looked at me. "Who else would do it? Who else is such a slime ball that they'd do something like this?"

"You're probably right but we can't prove it. And even if we could, I don't know if they'd do anything about it. It's a duck blind. I doubt that there are laws against burning a duck blind."

"Well legally we can't do anything but we can something. I will do something."

I didn't say anything knowing that when Noah was as angry as he was right now it wouldn't do any good anyway.

We stood there and watched as the floor burned until it fell apart and the charred wood fell into the river making a hiss as it hit the water. The only parts left on the trunk of the tree were the places where the lag bolts had held the wood in place. The bark on the tree was charred and a few of the close branches were blackened but it still looked ok for a blind.

"We've got plenty more wood," I said. "We can rebuild it."

Noah nodded. "But first we've got to settle this with Marco. If we re-build he'll just do the same thing unless we make it clear he's not going to get away with it."

Noah started for the boat and I followed. "You're not going to do anything stupid are you?"

He turned and looked at me. "I'm going to teach him a lesson."

"Noah..."

"Get in the boat!"

I got in and we took off upriver on the channel. It was much faster getting upriver if we kept to the channel rather than zigzagging back and forth on the backwaters. I knew where we were going and didn't like it but didn't say anything either. I was plenty mad at Marco but I didn't have the temper that Noah did.

Half an hour later we were above town and turned into a side channel that led to Gianolli's fish market. Noah pulled up to the dock. Marco's boat was tied up there. Noah got out and felt the cowling on the outboard and pulled his hand away. "It's hot, he just got back."

He started up the dock and Marco came out of the market wearing a rubber apron and gloves. "Who said you could come on our property Pederson?"

Noah didn't say a word. He strode up to Marco and before Marco could even put up his hands to defend himself, Noah hit him with a right punch and dropped him in his tracks on the gravel. Marco lay there for a second and shook his head and started to get up but then thought better of it.

Noah had his fist cocked back ready to smack Marco again and was just waiting for the chance to do it.

"You can't come here and hit me and get away with it," Marco said, blood running from his mouth. "I'm calling the sheriff."

"Good, go call him and we'll see what he has to say about you stealing our fish and burning down our duck blind, yeah Marco, go call him!"

Just then Marco's dad came from the market and walked up. "What's going on?" he said to Marco.

"Pederson came on our property and hit me in the mouth," he said.

Mr. Gianolli looked at Noah. "Can you tell me why you hit my son?"

"Yes I can Mr. Gianolli. Your son is a dirt bag. He's been stealing fish from our traps all summer and he burnt down our duck blind just now. He's a lying bastard and if he gets up I'm going to knock him down again."

Mr. Gianolli looked at Marco. "Is this true?"

"Of course not, I was out fishing."

"Is it true that you've touched their nets?"

"He's lying Pop."

"Ask him how he got covered with paint a while back," I said.

"He said he was helping a friend to paint a shed," Mr. Gianolli said.

"He was stealing fish from our nets. We rigged a booby trap to catch him and the dumb ox fell for it. Ask Julio he knows what Marco's been doing."

I could see Julio looking out the window of the market. "Julio, come out here," I said.

Julio walked out and looked at his brother. "Is this true?" his father asked.

Julio looked at the ground.

"Julio, I asked you a question."

"Did you burn their duck blind Marco?" Julio asked.

"No they're lying."

Julio shook his head. "Marco was stealing fish from their nets Pa. I was with him but he said he'd beat me if I told."

"You liar! It was your idea."

"Marco shut up. Not one more word," his father said.

Mr. Gianolli turned to us. "How much do we owe you for the fish he stole and the material for the blind?"

"You don't owe us anything Mr. Gianolli. We have no idea how many fish he took and the blind material was from our old smoker so it was free. All we had in it was our labor."

"I'll help you re-build it," Julio said.

"There, that's all we need for repayment," I said.

Mr. Gianolli nodded. "You won't be bothered by Marco again."

We shook hands with Mr. Gianolli and turned to the dock. "Julio, we'll talk to you in school tomorrow and make plans for working on the blind later in the week." Then Noah looked right at Marco still sitting on the ground with blood all over his nose and chin. "And if Julio shows up with even a tiny little mark on him, I'll be back."

"Ok, see you tomorrow," the younger boy said smiling.

"Marco... in the fish house," his father said.

Marco looked miserable as he got to his feet and shuffled off to the fish cleaning house. We didn't stay to watch what was going to happen but we were pretty sure it wasn't going to be much fun for Marco.

CHAPTER 15

WE WERE HEADING DOWNRIVER again at a much slower speed than we'd been going when Noah was driving us toward Gianolli's fish market.

"It'll be ok Noah," I said. "We've got plenty of wood and enough time to rebuild the blind. Julio said he'd help us so we don't have to worry about not getting it done before duck season opens."

"I know," he said. "It just makes me so damn mad to think that dope had to do that. What kind of person does something like that?"

I shrugged. "I don't know but the world's full of dopes and all we can do is let them be dopey and go on with life. Besides, we've got the experience of the first blind so the new one will be even easier to build. And... this way we can get to know Julio."

Noah rocked his head from side to side. "Yeah, I guess we'll be ok. Still makes me mad though."

When we got back to Noah's his dad had the crappies all cleaned. He asked us what had happened and we told him about the blind and our little encounter with Marco. We left out the part about him stealing fish. We figured that if he didn't know about that it would probably be for the best. Steffen was pretty calm but if he knew about Marco messing with his nets he might not take it too well.

The next day when we got to school Julio was standing by our lockers waiting. He looked uncomfortable when we walked up. "I hope you guys know I wasn't in on burning your blind," he said.

I nodded. "We never thought it was you Julio."

"I don't know what's wrong with Marco," he said. "Sometimes he acts like such a mutt. When are you planning on going out to work on the blind?"

"We thought we'd haul out a load of wood after school. Are you busy?"

"Nope, I'll walk down with you guys and help until it's all done."

We nodded and shook hands with Julio and the three of us went off to class.

After school the three of us walked first to my house so I could change into some work clothes and then down to Noah's. Noah loaned Julio some old jeans and a tee shirt to work in and we walked down to the boat landing and loaded up a boat full of wood. We called the dogs and all of us got in the boat and motored out to the island. The dogs took off playing and the three of us unloaded the lumber.

"Let's tear off the last pieces of the burnt stuff," I said.

Noah and I walked out onto the bridge and began prying off the burnt ends of the boards. Julio climbed down to the depression that the roots of the tree had created when it toppled over into the river.

"I'll climb out onto the tree and pull that burnt stuff off," he said as he stepped into the mud at the edge of the depression. He took about one step and his feet slid out from under him and down he went into the mud hole. "Whoa!" he yelled as he slid up to his mid-belly.

We looked down and began to laugh. "Holy crap," he said. "That hole is a lot deeper than it looks."

The hole was full of water and he'd thought it was just a little mud puddle. We knew it was deep but had failed to tell Julio about it.

"When the tree came out of the ground it made a big hole," I said laughing at Julio standing there in the mud."

"No kidding," Julio said looking up at us. "I'm stuck like a plug in a sink."

Noah and I lay down on the bridge and held our arms down to Julio and he took hold of them and we pulled and he finally slipped up and out of the mud. He swung his feet over to the side of the hole and we let him drop.

"Holy smokes, that was a bad idea," he said. "Maybe you guys will think I'm not much help if I do stuff like that."

We laughed. "Maybe you'll change your idea about helping us," I said.

"Naw, I'm gonna jump in the river and get this mud off me or I'll make a real mess of the boat on the way back."

Julio took off his shoes and socks and dove into the river. He swam around wiping off mud and the whole river turned brown around him. After a while he climbed out looking much less brown than he had earlier. "Well, I'm not clean but cleaner," he said.

"As long as you're down there, you might as well still get all that burned wood off the tree," Noah said.

"No problem," Julio said climbing up onto the trunk. He pried off the board ends and tossed them into the river while we finished up on the bridge. I tossed the wrench across to him and he backed out the lag bolts and put them in his pocket so we could use them again. When we were finished we still had our bridge and an open spot to begin re-building our blind.

"Well, let's head home," I said.

"We can go upriver and drop you off Julio," Noah said.

"That'd be great," he said.

On the way upriver Julio smiled at me and said. "I'm glad you guys are letting me help. When I go and do stuff with Marco it's no fun. At least you guys have fun."

"You're welcome with us any time Julio. Just leave your mutt brother at home."

Julio grinned and gave me a thumbs-up. "That's a deal," he said.

CHAPTER 16

THE FOLLOWING DAY we walked home after classes and Julio went with us again to the blind. This time we took some tools and nails along and with me cutting boards to length and Julio and Noah nailing them together we had the floor and two walls finished by time to go home.

"Why don't you stay over tonight Julio?" I said. "We don't have school tomorrow so we can go out and probably finish all the construction... that is unless you have plans."

"I'd love to stay over. I had no plans for tomorrow except maybe fishing and this is more fun than going fishing with Marco," he said.

"When we get home you can call your parents and let them know," I said.

We motored back to the dock and tied up the boat, took the tools up to the fish market and then Noah grabbed some clean clothes and we all walked up to my house. When we got there I told Gram of our plans and she was happy to have Julio as a guest.

"I was just peeling potatoes so I'll throw in a few extra. I have chicken in the oven and two fresh apple pies cooling, so there will be plenty of food for all of you."

Julio was beaming. "My ma isn't much of a cook," he said. "I do most of the cooking at home. My dad taught me a few things and he likes my cooking better than ma's. This'll be a treat to get fed like this without me doing all the work."

We went upstairs and took turns having a bath and then

changed into clean clothes. I loaned Julio some extra stuff and we all went down for supper when Gram called us. The table was filled with wonderful smelling food and Mom was home so we sat and had a grand supper. Afterward the three of us cleaned up the kitchen and did dishes while Gram and Mom sat on the porch enjoying a beautiful evening.

"I can't remember a fall like this for a long time," Gram said.

"Me either, we really haven't had a good frost yet and it's nearly the end of October already. A very strange year," Mom said.

After supper we walked into town and went to the gas station and got a bottle of pop and sat and chatted with some of the local guys. The talk turned to duck hunting which was opening the next Saturday morning.

"I don't think we'll have much of a season," an old timer said. "All the ducks I've seen in the last few weeks are just a few local mallards and a couple of teal. Once in a while you see a wood duck but there aren't many of them either. Been too warm, all the ducks are still in Canada."

A pickup pulled into the gas station and an old man got out of it to get some gas. The attendant came out and began washing his window and when he got to the truck an old white faced golden retriever stuck her head out of the window and sniffed him.

"Hey look, that's that old guy we almost ran over," I said.

"Let's go apologize," Noah said.

We walked over to the old man who was getting a bottle of pop and he turned toward us. "Ah, the boys who were in a big hurry," he said smiling.

"We're really sorry sir," I said.

"We were trying to get out by the channel to put out a fire in our duck blind," Noah said.

"Your duck blind? How did your duck blind get on fire?"

"It's kind of a long story but we were too late anyway. We're rebuilding it now.'

The old man giggled. "Strange things happen to duck hunters," he said.

"Well we did want to tell you we're sorry for almost hitting you," I said.

"No problem apology accepted. I think my old dog Bea is probably willing to let it go too."

"I have a golden too," I said. "Her name is Kate."

"Bea has been my friend for thirteen years. She's not too spry any more but she still likes to go along. We're both getting too old for the river but we're too cantankerous to give it up."

The man paid for the gas and said goodbye and left.

The old timer who we'd been talking with said, "Old Harry knows ducks. I bet if you'd have asked him he'd tell you the same thing. They're going to be scarce this year."

"They'll come one of these days," Noah said.

"Oh sure they'll come, but if the weather stays this warm, it'll be after the season is all over and we've put away our guns for the winter."

The three of us looked at each other. "I hope we're not wasting our time building this blind," I said.

"Don't worry," Noah said, "It'll be worth it.....just wait and see."

We finished up our pop and walked back to my house. We said goodnight to Mom and Gram and went up to my room. I had a fold up cot in the closet and we made that up and Julio laid down on it. Noah shared my double bed with Kate and Karen and me.

"Jeez this bed is pretty full," Noah said trying to move Kate off his legs.

Kate looked up at him and moaned. "I don't think she likes the idea of you in HER bed," I said laughing.

"Kate, my love," he said scratching her head. "Move your large carcass over a bit will you?"

Kate rolled over a little and Noah straightened out his long legs. He looked at me and mimed shooting a gun into the air and then pointed at Julio and shrugged.

I knew what he was getting at. "Hey Julio, as long as you're helping build the blind, do you want to hunt with us?"

"Really? That would be great if you guys don't mind. I'm not the best shot in the world but I'd love to hunt with you guys."

"We're not experts either but we'll have the most comfortable blind on the river and it's sure big enough for all three of us," Noah said.

"Wow, I can't wait," Julio said.

I smiled at Noah who was grinning. "Well tomorrow we'll get out there and probably finish it up. Then this week we need to get our stuff ready and next Saturday we'll be ready for action."

It was going to be a duck season to remember.

CHAPTER 17

THE NEXT MORNING we had a huge breakfast and Gram made us a bag of sandwiches for lunch. She wrapped up three slices of apple pie and put in a thermos of milk and we headed down to the dock to load the last pieces of lumber that we needed.

We took off for the blind with the dogs in the bow, their ears flying in the wind. Noah was pushing the boat pretty hard and we came around a blind corner in the channel and right in our path was the old man from town in a little row boat with the old retriever in the front of the boat sitting on the front seat. Noah yelled, "Whoa!" and turned the boat hard to the left to avoid hitting the man. When he turned so sharply the boat threw a huge wave right at the side of the old man and his boat. The wave washed over the side and the boat was filled with water immediately.

Noah cut the throttle back and we coasted to a stop but when we looked back the old man was in the water and his boat was barely staying up. I pulled off my shoes and dove over the side of our boat and began swimming toward the old man and Julio did the same and went in and swam to his boat. He was paddling around and looked kind of dazed when I got to him. His dog was swimming toward shore.

"Are you ok?" I said.

"Well, I fell out of my boat but otherwise I'm just ducky," the old guy said.

I laughed and he grinned at me. "You guys in a big hurry?"

"I'm sorry sir, we were going too fast, can I help you to shore?"

"I can swim, you help your partner rescue my boat and try not to lose my fishing poles from it eh?"

I watched as he dog paddled to the shore. His dog crawled up on dry ground and shook herself off and then stood there watching us with her tail wagging. I swam over and helped Julio push the flooded little boat to shore. When we got there Noah had nosed the front of our boat up onto the land and was helping the old man out of the water.

"I'm so sorry, are you ok?" he said.

"Nothing but a little wet," he old man said. He called the dog over and ruffled her ears. "Old Bea here wanted to take a swim anyway, didn't you old girl?" The dog's tail wagged furiously.

Julio and I got his boat to the bank and tipped it to get some of the water out and then when it was lighter we lifted it up onto land and dumped the rest out. There were two fishing poles in the boat and a coffee can full of mud that was probably also full of fish worms. I took the can out and dumped it into the grass and sorted his worms out of the mud. I filled the can with dry grass and put it back into the boat.

"So where are you boys going in such a hurry?" the old man said. "Is your blind on fire again?"

We all stood there feeling kind of bad but had to grin. The old fart was pretty tough even though he looked to be about eighty years old. "We're finishing up our duck blind today and were kind of in a hurry to get started," I said.

"Duck season doesn't open until Saturday," he said.

"Yeah, we know," Noah said. "I wasn't thinking I'm real sorry. Can we make it up to you some way Mr.....?"

"Gillette, Harry Gillette," he said.

"Well Mr. Gillette, what can we do to make up for being so stupid?" I said.

Gillette laughed. "It's not stupid to be in a hurry to build a duck blind. I've built many of them in my day and I enjoyed every minute of it. Duck hunting is a great sport. I've been hunting them for over sixty years."

"Wow," I said. "You must have a million stories."

Gillette laughed again. "Son I have two million and the ducks get bigger and the shots longer every time I tell them."

The only one of us who wasn't wet was Noah and the rest of us were shivering a bit in the early morning coolness. "Let's go back and get our clothes dried out and then we can start over," I said.

"Mr. Gillette would you like to come with us and get dried off?" Noah asked.

"That I would," he said. "Maybe we can tell some duck stories while we wait."

We left Mr. Gillette's stuff on the river bank and he got into the big boat with the three of us and the dogs. Kate and Karen were very interested in the new person and he seemed to like them a lot too. His old dog and our two seemed like they were old friends immediately. When we got back to the fish market, we walked up and Noah got dry clothes for the two of us and some overalls and a shirt from his grandpa for Mr. Gillette. We all changed in the smoker house and we hung our wet clothes on a clothes line.

Noah's grandpa seemed to know Mr. Gillette and soon they were chatting and drinking coffee. We decided to eat our lunch while we waited and shared it with Mr. Gillette since his was water logged in the bottom of his boat.

"What do you think the shooting will be like on Saturday?" I asked.

"Won't be much," Gillette said.

"You don't think so?"

"Weather's been too nice. All we have around here are the local ducks that nested here. There's not many of them for all the hunters who'll be out on that river. And once those ducks get shot at a few times they'll skedaddle up into the hills to some ponds and creeks. We need some nasty weather in the north to push of those northern ducks down here."

"Well, we've got our blind in a place where we can fish if things get slow," Noah said grinning.

"Is that your hotel in that tree out by the channel?" Mr. Gillette asked.

"Hotel?" I said. "That's a deluxe duck blind."

Mr. Gillette grinned. "You boys are really gonna rough it aren't you?"

I shrugged, "We might as well be comfortable."

Gillette nodded. "Have you got both diving duck decoys and puddle duck decoys?"

We all looked kind of befuddled. "We don't have any decoys," Noah said.

"Oh I see," he said. "I suppose the ducks are going to just fly past your hotel there because they think it looks so inviting?"

I looked at Julio and Noah. "We didn't think about decoys. We've been thinking about the blind."

"I hunt pretty light now days," Mr. Gillette said. "I just take half a dozen decoys with me and hunt from the boat. My knees aren't what they used to be so I don't wade much. I've got some extra decoys in the shed out back of my place that won't get used this year...unless you guys want to use them."

"What? Are you serious?" I said.

"Well they're not doing anyone any good sitting in a shed."

"Yeah but after we almost ran over you, you'd do that for us?" Noah asked.

Gillette grinned. "Maybe if the weather turns a bit you'll let me sit in your hotel some day with you."

We were all grins. "You'd be welcome any day Mr. Gillette."

CHAPTER 18

WE TOOK MR. GILLETTE back to his boat and helped him get it back into the water.

"You guys come over later in the week and get some of those decoys then," he said. "If you're on the river, take the channel just past the mile marker where the railroad runs right next to the river. You can park at my dock and we can load the decoys right into your boat."

"That's really generous of you Mr. Gillette," I said. "seeing as how we almost drowned you earlier."

He laughed. "It'll take more than you young whippersnappers to drown an old river rat like me. It was a good adventure and now I have another story to add to my long list of tales."

We decided to meet him on Wednesday after school and off we went toward our blind. As we pulled away I grinned as the old man began rowing his little boat toward some grass beds in the next cut. He probably didn't want to waste those worms he had in his boat.

When we got to the blind we unloaded the tools and Noah and Julio climbed out onto the blind and started giving me measurements for boards. I cut the planks off and tossed them up to them and in no time we had the rest of the walls finished. We'd bought some new hinges and a clasp for the roof. With both Julio and Noah nailing boards and me cutting them it didn't take long to get the roof finished. We put the new hinges and hasp on it and it was just getting dusk when we finished. Noah locked it down with a stick through the hasp on the inside and then we did the same with the back door.

"Do you think we should get a lock for it?" I asked.

"I don't think anyone else would touch it do you?" Noah said.

"No I think most hunters or fishermen would respect it and keep their hands off."

"Not Marco," Julio said.

"You think he'll come back?"

"No I doubt it," he said after thinking about it for a minute. "Pa gave him a whooping. I don't think he'd want to take a chance on another of those."

We all laughed and rounded up the dogs and piled into the boat. It was pretty dark by the time we got back so we hurried up and put the tools away and then tied up the boat and Noah gassed it up so his dad could go check his fish traps the next morning.

"I'll see you guys in school," Julio said and he took off walking toward town and his house.

"See ya in the morning," I said and headed home myself with Kate galloping along beside me.

The next day after school we put some new tin on the roof and finished up all the little extra things to make the blind comfortable. We made some little stools to sit on and made a box for lunch and extra stuff. Then we made sure all the cracks were closed up by nailing strips of tar paper over them. "Might as well make it tight," I said. "If we get a windy day it'll be a lot nicer inside if we don't have wind blowing in through those cracks."

The following day we went and cut grass to make new mats for the outside of the blind. We'd measured all the sides and roof and when we had a boat full of cattails and tall grass we took it back to the landing and began making our mat. Again, with three of us working it took a lot less time. Having a extra person helping made things go faster. The fact that Noah and I had already done this once helped too because this time we knew just what we were doing. As we got more and more mat made we rolled it up into several rolls so when we got to the blind we could just unroll them and tack them to the outside of the blind. It was gonna be one cool blind.

We finished up the mats and stacked them to the side of the dock where they'd be out of the way. "Tomorrow we'll run up to

Mr. Gillette's and get some decoys," I said.

Noah nodded. "That'll be cool to have a few decoys, I didn't even think about that. I'm used to hiding in the weeds and shooting at any ducks that come too close. This should be a lot more fun to have some actually come in to us.'

Julio and I agreed. "I'm not much of a shot but I think if they're trying to land in by some decoys they'll be a lot easier to hit than if they're going past about a hundred miles an hour," he said.

Noah began laughing. "Last year Sebastian took a shot at a string of little ducks that we thought were teal that were coming over the weeds. He said, 'I'm gonna bust that leader." He shot and the fourth duck back dropped out of the sky."

Julio laughed. "They go pretty fast don't they?"

I nodded. "No kidding. I had no idea they were moving that fast. But from now on I'm not going to make any prediction which duck I'm shooting at. If one falls I'm taking credit as the one I was shooting at."

The closer we got to opening day the more excited we were getting. I could hardly wait until tomorrow after school to get a few decoys. We just might actually get some ducks this year.

I was hoping that Mr. Gillette would also give us some advice on hunting ducks since our experience was pretty thin. He seemed to be willing to help us since he offered to let us use some decoys. A guy who had hunted for 60 years had probably seen it all and knew exactly what to do and when to do it...and we planned on listening to him pretty closely for advice.

CHAPTER 19

IT SEEMED LIKE THE DAY was never going to end Wednesday at school. Every time classes changed we'd see Julio and glance at the clock knowing we were just a bit closer to getting out onto the river to meet Mr. Gillette. When the final bell rang we hurried down to my house and Julio and I changed clothes. He'd left some work clothes there so he didn't have to wear his good school clothes on the river. Then we went to Noah's and he changed and we headed out with the little boat for the river.

We followed the backwater cuts to the main channel and then went upriver until we saw the mile marker by the railroad tracks and turned into the cut that ran past it. We twisted and turned following the narrow channel and finally came around the bend and saw a small dock and a cottage on the river bank. The cottage looked like something from a picture postcard. It was built of logs and had a big screened front porch. There was a natural stone chimney coming up the side and there was a little curl of smoke wafting up out of it. Behind the cottage was a large shed made of corrugated steel. Mr. Gillette's row boat was sitting in the water at the dock and we pulled up and Julio tied us up. We got out and walked up onto the lawn and Mr. Gillette came out of the house.

"Hello boys, come on up and let's take a look at those decoys," he said.

We followed him around the house to the shed. The shed also had a garage door so we figured it must have once been used as a garage. Mr. Gillette opened the door and we followed him inside.

"Wow," Noah said as he saw the inside.

"Holy smokes, decoys," I said.

We'd expected to see a few dozen decoys sitting on a shelf or in a burlap bag but what we saw was amazing. There were shelves from floor to ceiling along all the walls and each shelf was packed full of duck decoys. There were hundreds of them. They looked like many different species of ducks, many of which I'd never seen before.

Mr. Gillette chuckled. "I've been collecting decoys all my life and I guess I might have a few more than most folks," he said.

We spread out with our mouths agape looking at all the different types of ducks that were portrayed in wood. I had no idea there were so many kinds of ducks before this.

"Mr. Gillette, where did you get all of these?"

"Well, you boys have to remember I'm an old man and I've been collecting them for a long time. I bought my first ones back when I was about your age from a local carver and then over the years I've just been collecting them as I found new ones that I didn't have. There was a company in Michigan named Mason Decoys that made them from the late 1800's to 1924 and many of these are that brand. Others I just found in shops or bought at estate sales as old hunters died."

"I didn't know there were so many kinds of ducks, let alone decoys," Noah said.

"There are two specific types of ducks boys, puddle ducks and diving ducks, did you know that?"

We shook our heads. "Well," he continued, "the puddle ducks are the ones most people know and see more often. The best known is the mallard. Everyone knows them because they're everywhere and there are a lot of tame ones that you see in parks and on farms. Another that is pretty common is the wood duck. It makes its home in small ponds with woods around them. Wood ducks nest in hollow trees so they live near their homes.

"I know teal," I said. "They're like little rockets."

Mr. Gillette laughed. "Did you know there are three types of teal?"

I shook my head. He walked over to a shelf with little decoys sitting on it. He picked up one with green wing patches. "This one is a green wing teal it's the smallest duck and one of the fastest flyers. A full grown green wing only weighs about 6 ounces...a pretty small bird. This is his cousin the blue winged teal. They're a bit larger and have a blue wing patch. There's also one called cinnamon teal," he said picking up a reddish decoy. "They're not as common but are around now and then."

"Holy smokes, how do you tell them all apart?" Noah said.

"The males are easy," Mr. Gillette said, "but the females look pretty much all alike. In fact most all female puddle ducks are grey mottled ducks. The differences are in foot color, eye color, and sometimes feather shape."

The three of us stood there totally confused. "So how do we know what we have?"

"Practice boys," he said giggling.

We moved through the shed and Mr. Gillette showed us examples of other puddle ducks like a gadwall which looked to my eyes exactly like a hen mallard. We saw widgeon decoys, pintails, and one called a black duck that looked like a really dark mallard hen.

"Boy, I had no idea there was this much to learn," I said.

Mr. Gillette grinned. "We've just covered the puddle ducks boys, we still have the diving ducks to learn and they're even more difficult to identify."

"Puddle ducks, and diving ducks?" Julio said.

Puddle ducks are built different," Mr. Gillette said. "Their feet are more centered under their body and they have large wings. They can walk on land easily, like how the mallards at the park waddle up and beg food. They can also take off from a sitting position on the water. They can jump into the air and fly away. Diving ducks legs are farther back on their body so they can't walk on land very well. Their wings are smaller too so they have to flap their wings and 'run' on the top of the water to get enough speed to take off."

"I've seen ducks do that," I said. "I thought they were just having fun."

Mr. Gillette laughed. "I suppose it is fun but that's the only way they can fly.

We moved to another part of the shed and Mr. Gillette began showing us the diving duck decoys. We started with the scaup. It turned out that there were two ducks called scaup which were commonly called blue bills.

"There is a lesser and a greater scaup," Mr. Gillette said. We groaned.

"How do you tell them apart?" Julio asked.

"One is larger than the other. It's pretty hard to tell unless you have one of each side by side. I wouldn't worry about it boys," Mr. Gillette said grinning.

Then we saw golden eyes, buffle heads, red heads, and what he called the king of ducks, the canvasback. We were totally baffled by now.

I looked at Noah and Julio and said, "Maybe we're not ready for this."

Mr. Gillette laughed. "Don't worry boys. I'll give you a few pointers and you'll do fine. The thing is that each of these ducks will come down from the north at a different time of the fall. The teal are fair weather ducks. They begin to migrate as soon as it begins to frost. Then the wood ducks go and then gadwalls, widgeon and mallards. The divers come next and the last to come will be buffle heads and golden eyes. It's not that hard."

"When they're flying how do you know what you're shooting at?" Noah asked.

"That's simple," he said. "Every kind of duck has a kind of pattern they fly in. All you have to do it learn to identify them by their wing beat and flying patterns. Some fly in nice orderly V's. Some fly in loose formations and some fly in no formation at all but just scramble around in loose flocks. Wood ducks look down at the ground and then back up all the time. As you see ducks coming and then bag one, you can remember what they looked like in the air and the next time you'll know what's flying your way."

My head was beginning to ache.

CHAPTER 20

WE LISTENED WHILE Mr. Gillette told us of the different flight patterns that each type of duck had and he told us things like watching their heads and how they held them and how their wing beats differed. It was all very confusing to three boys who up until then thought that a duck was a duck.

"Let's go up to the house and have some hot chocolate and we can talk some more," Mr. Gillette said.

We followed him into the house and again our mouths fell open. There were ducks, deer heads, a wild boar head, and even a moose head hanging from the walls. There were dozens of fish and a fox mounted on a tree limb.

"Holy smokes, Mr. Gillette, this is like a museum," I said.

He laughed. "I told you boys, I've been hunting and fishing for a long time, I've collected a lot of junk over the years. And boys, please call me Harry, my father was Mr. Gillette."

We grinned and nodded. "Sit down and I'll get some milk heating."

We sat at a big table and just looked around us at all the marvelous trophies hanging on the walls. Harry came back into the living room and started telling us what kind of ducks each one was and sometimes a little story about how he'd happened to get it.

"This mallard drake was the first I ever got that was a big mature one," he said. "See these curly little feathers above the tail? They mean this guy was an old duck, he has four curls. They don't get curls on their back until they're at least a couple of years old. My old dog and I snuck up on this guy and a hen one evening just at dusk. We saw them land in a puddle a little way from us and we crawled through the marsh until we were close enough to shoot. I got them both and the dog retrieved them. It was one of the prettiest hunts I ever had. I was about 19 years old. I had never shot a mature drake mallard like that so I decided to have it mounted to be able to relive the hunt. It cost eight dollars to have it stuffed. I didn't have eight dollars so I offered to work it off at the taxidermists. I worked 6 months cleaning up and helping skin animals but I got my duck."

He smiled to himself as he relived the story.

"How long ago was that Harry?" Julio asked.

"It was a long time ago Julio, over sixty years ago.....a very long time ago. Each time I got a new species of duck after that I had it stuffed. I worked off quite a few of them and then finally made enough money that I could just pay for them. He looked around the room at all of his trophies and smiled. "They each have a story," he said.

"Don't tell us you got that moose someplace around here," I said.

Harry laughed. "No I know you guys aren't that green. I went to Alaska many years ago and shot that big guy. It was the first time I'd ever flown in a plane. We flew back into a lake that was a hundred miles from the closest road and they left me and my hunting companions there. I shot that big moose and it took us three days to cut the thing up and haul it back to the outpost. They take a chainsaw and put cooking oil in place of bar oil and cut the things up out in the swamp. I almost wished I'd never have shot the darn thing after I found out how much work it was going to be to get it out. So I decided to have the head mounted to remind me of the trip."

Noah looked at me and grinned. He knew either of us would probably do the same thing. Outdoor memories were something we also cherished.

Harry went back to the kitchen and came back with a tray with four steaming mugs of hot chocolate and a plate of cookies.

"Baked them myself," he said.

"Where did you get that wild boar Harry?" Noah asked.

"Right out on the river," Harry said.

We all looked surprised and then Harry broke out laughing. "No I'm just kidding. I shot that beast down in Texas in 1910. Blasted critter," he said, "I was hunting deer on the ranch of a friend of mine who came up here duck hunting for many years. In Texas they make blinds and sit and shoot at deer at long distances as they pass the blinds. We were sitting there and I heard this critter grunt and thought my friend had farted. We were arguing about that and the boar crashed into the back of the blind and damn near ran us over. My friend got knocked through the front wall of the blind. I managed to get up and turn and shot the beast from about two feet."

We listened enthralled as Harry told us stories for almost two hours and then we noticed it was getting dark outside. "We better get going," Noah said. "We've got the boat and it'll take us a while to get all the way back to our dock."

"I didn't realize how late it was getting," Harry said. "Why don't you leave the boat here and I'll haul you guys home. I'll pick you up after school tomorrow at the fish market and bring you back to get the boat."

That sounded like a plan to us so Noah and I got into the back of the pickup and Julio sat up front. Harry dropped Julio off and then took us to the fish market.

"Thanks a million Harry," I said.

"No problem boys, it was fun having someone to talk to. See you tomorrow."

Harry drove off into the night. "He's quite a guy," Noah said.

"No kidding. He's been an outdoorsman for his whole life. I'm amazed at how much he knows about stuff."

"I wonder if we'll be that smart when we're like eighty years old?"

"Jeez, that's a long way from now. You think we'll ever be eighty?"

I shrugged. "I hope so. At least if I could be as spry as Harry, I'd sure like to live to see eighty. Well see you tomorrow."

I walked home and got ready for bed. As I lay there with Kate snuggled up to me snoring I thought of all that Harry must have seen and experienced in all those years of hunting and fishing. What a lucky guy he was to have done all that and lived so long.

I was thinking about the opening of duck season in a few days on Saturday as I drifted off to sleep.

CHAPTER 21

WHEN WE WALKED out the front door of the school the next day Harry was sitting in the parking lot of the school waiting for us. His dog Bea was sitting in the passenger seat. "You guys want to run home and change clothes first?" he asked.

"Naw, we'll just be careful and wear these," Noah said.

"Hop in," Harry said.

Bea didn't offer to move over so we piled in back and Harry drove us down the street to his house. When we got there we saw that the boat had several bags of decoys in it. "I took the liberty of loading a few decoys for you guys," Harry said.

We walked down to the boat. "Open that sack up," Harry said.

I pulled the string off the first bag and looked inside. "Those are teal, both blue wing and green wing. They often fly and feed together so I gave you five blues and 6 greens."

I looked at Harry. "Why eleven?"

Harry shrugged. "It's an old superstition of mine. You buy decoys by the dozen usually and these ducks get used to seeing twelve of their cousins sitting on the water and then they get shot at, I think it's better not to have an even dozen."

I didn't know whether to laugh of not. "You mean you think they can count?"

"Never hurts to be careful," he said with a twinkle in his eye.

We all giggled and I opened the next bag. In it were seven wood ducks and three coots. Harry explained that the coots were confidence decoys. They often hung around in the same ponds as ducks and having a few in your decoy set made it look more natural. The next bag had eight mallards and five pintails in it.

"Those are all puddle ducks and all will be together many times. When you put them out put them on the marsh side of your blind, in by the cattails and lily pads. Set them out in little family groups and leave some room between them for the real ducks to land if they come in."

We all nodded that we understood.

"There are lead weights on each of the cords that are hooked to the bottom of each duck so be sure to put them in shallow water so they're able to 'swim' when the breeze blows. It makes them look more realistic."

"Thanks Harry, we wouldn't have had a clue if it wasn't for you," I said.

"No problem boys. Oh one more thing, when you set them out make sure they're crowded on the outside so the open space is nearer to you. That way the ducks won't try to land out too far and out of your gun range."

"Geez Harry, maybe you should come with us. Then we'd be sure to get it right."

"Oh I've got a little spot upriver a way that I like to sit at on opening day. Old Bea and I will be just fine there. I'll check with you guys sometime afterward. You'll do just fine. Just put the decoys out and sit tight. Which one of you does the calling?"

We all looked at each other.

"None of you knows how to call ducks?" Harry asked.

"All we've ever done is stand in the tall grass and shoot at ducks that fly past close enough," I said.

"I've never shot a duck," Julio said. "I'm going for the first time."

"Oh boy," Harry said. "We better go up to the house, I'm going to have to give you guys a few calling lessons."

We all grinned at each other. Man, we really had no clue what we were doing did we? Julio said, "And I thought I was getting to go hunting with some experienced duck hunters."

Noah laughed. "Shut up Julio."

We got to Harry's house and we went into the living room. Harry opened a cupboard and came out with a cardboard box and sat it on the table. He took the lid off and it was nearly full of duck calls. "Holy smokes Harry, you think you got enough of those things?" Noah said his eyes bugging out.

"Like I said boys, I've collected a lot of stuff in my lifetime. Every time someone came out with a new duck call I thought I needed to try one. Consequently I've got quite a few of them.

"Are they all for the same kind of duck or what?" I said.

"Most are mallard calls. Mallards are the most common duck and almost any other kind of duck will come to their call. I have some wood duck calls and a pintail call but they're no big deal."

He picked up a call and put it in his mouth and blew into it. It sounded like "Waaaa waaa waa waa waa." He did it again. "That's a hail call. It means 'Hey, what's up? If you're not doing anything stop in and say hi.'"

We laughed. "That's what it means?"

Harry grinned. "Hen mallards are the gossip girls of the duck world. They're friends with everyone and always looking for someone to chat with. This is the way they say hi."

Then he took the call and made a gabbling sound with it. It sounded like "Chucka chucka, chucka chucka."

"That's a feeding call. When a mallard is eating they make that sound. They tell other ducks that are flying overhead, 'Hey, we've got chow here, come on down and join us.'"

Again we all giggled. "So we've got to learn to do that?" I said.

Harry nodded. "Those two calls and one more will be all you need. The other is the comeback call. If some ducks come past and don't stop, you need to plead with them to come back. He put the call in his mouth and made a sound that sounded like, 'Waaaaaaaaa waa waa waa." It was very similar to the hail call but more pleading.

"Here try," he said handing Noah the call. Noah put it in his mouth and blew on it. The sound sounded like a long juicy fart. We all laughed and Harry just about fell off his chair.

"Put a little more oomph in it."

Noah tried again and it sounded faintly like Harry's hail call. "Again."

Noah kept at it and soon his hail call was sounding pretty good. "Now try the comeback call. Just make it more pleading."

Noah did it and it sounded good on the first try. He grinned when we pronounced him our official caller.

"Wait, you've got to master the feeding call. That's the hard one."

"When you blow the feeding call, you try to say in the back of your mouth, ta-ka, ta-ka, ta-ka, ta-ka. Try it."

Noah blew on the call and it was awful. We laughed and he tried again. This time it sounded a little like Harry's feeding call. He tried it again and again and it began to sound like the call Harry had made.

"Just keep practicing that one," Harry said. "You won't master it over night but you'll get it."

He rummaged around in the box and pulled out two more calls. He handed one to me and one to Julio. "That one is another mallard call. You guys should all try to learn to call. Sometimes two calls are better than one. The other is a goose call in case a flock of geese comes by. I'll give you some goose decoys later in the season but you guys should practice your calling before you start to hunt."

We all picked up our calls and began blowing on them. It sounded like someone was killing a bunch of cats. Harry laughed. "Take them home with you, drive your folks nuts."

We thanked Harry and loaded up in the boat and started off downriver. There were quite a few stares by people in other boats as we went past blowing our duck calls. They probably thought we'd lost our minds.

CHAPTER 22

WE HAD TWO DAYS left to get everything ready for the opening of the duck season on Saturday. The day after Harry lent us the decoys we took them out to the blind and stored them inside. We made a few finishing touches on the grass and branches we'd used to camouflage the blind and added a little dull black paint to any places that looked too shiny. On Friday we all went to my house after school and made a bunch of sandwiches and wrapped up some cookies and other goodies into a large cloth bag for our lunch on Saturday.

"Are you guys going for a week or just tomorrow?" Gram asked as she came into the kitchen and saw our heap of food.

"This is just for tomorrow Gram," Noah said. "You better bake some more bread tomorrow we'll probably need more for Sunday."

Gram just shook her head. "I swear, it would be cheaper to buy ducks than to feed you guys so you can go shoot some."

Noah and I each had a pair of hip boots so we put them into the pile of gear on the back porch. Julio had some regular low rubber boots but it was ok because we really didn't have to get out into the water to put the decoys out so he could just stay in the boat or at the blind. The hip boots were there just in case we had to get out in the grass to look for a duck or had problems where one of us had to get into the water. We ate supper with Mom and Gram and then went up to my room to get our guns and ammo ready.

Julio had a single shot 16gauge shotgun and his dad had given him two boxes of shells. Noah and I each had a 12 gauge and between us we'd bought 3 boxes so we had 125 shells between the three of us. "If we can't get a couple of dozen ducks with 125 shells, we'd better go back to squirrel hunting," I said.

"We'll get lots more than that," Noah said. "We've got all the best stuff we can have. Our blind is perfect. We've got Harry's decoys and calls, what could go wrong?"

Julio and I looked at each other and grinned.

That night it was hard to get to sleep. Julio was sleeping on the cot and Karen had decided to sleep with him. Kate was in the middle of the bed between Noah and me and she was restless too, like she knew something big was about to happen the next morning. Noah kept turning over and checking the alarm clock until at 5am he got up. "I can't stand it anymore," he said. "Let's get up, I know neither of you is sleeping."

I sat up in bed and Julio rolled over and grinned. "I've been awake for hours," he said.

"Well, let's get up and get ready and have some breakfast and then we can get out to the blind before the ducks wake up."

We took turns in the bathroom and soon we all were ready. Kate and Karen had gone downstairs ahead of us and were waiting in the kitchen. There was a wonderful smell coming up the stairway. Gram was up and had a stack of pancakes sitting in the middle of the table. "I knew you guys wouldn't be able to sleep, so I thought you should have a good breakfast before you headed out."

I smiled at the old lady and gave her a kiss on the cheek. "You're just like your Dad," she said. "He couldn't sleep before going hunting either."

I thought of my Dad and how he must be missing this day. He'd always been an avid hunter but the last couple of years he'd missed most of the hunting season with his work. He'd go and work for a month and then have one week off. This time of year they worked non-stop to get as many trips across the lake as possible before it iced up, so he hadn't been home for several weeks.

"I hope he gets home before the season is over," I said. "I bet he'll be impressed with our duck blind."

"Oh he'll love it," Gram said. "When he was about your age he and a friend built a duck blind and spent many years hunting from it. It was washed away in a big flood and I thought he was going to cry when he found it was gone. He'll want to go see your blind as soon as he gets home."

We all filled our bellies with pancakes and put on our boots and picked up our gear. We each had our gun and, Noah had the lunch sack and I carried a jug of water and thermos of hot chocolate. Julio brought the canvass bag with all the shotgun shells. We were loaded down pretty well.

"You guys be careful and don't shoot each other," Gram said as we trudged off into the dark morning.

"Have the hot water ready old woman. When we hunters get back you can pluck our ducks for us," Noah said over his shoulder.

Gram just laughed.

We walked down to the little boat which was all gassed up and ready and loaded our gear into it. The dogs jumped in and then Noah got in the back and started the motor. Julio sat in the middle with the Karen in his lap and I untied the rope and got into the bow. Kate stood in the bow with her feet up on the front seat and looked out into the night watching where we were going.

"Here we go," Noah said as he put the motor into gear. We headed into the darkness about as excited as three boys and two dogs could be.

CHAPTER 23

THE MOON HAD ALREADY SET so the only light we had was from the stars. It was a crystal clear night so navigating through the back channels to our blind wasn't too hard as long as we took it easy. Noah had made the trip so many times that he almost knew where to turn without looking.

Julio was sitting in the middle and Karen was on his lap, her little ears flapping in the breeze as she stared ahead. He was grinning from ear to ear. "You look like you're excited," I said. He nodded.

"I've never gotten to do much hunting before. Marco never let me go with him and I doubt it would have been much fun if I had. I've gone by myself a few times but that's not much fun. I just hope I don't screw it up for you guys."

I laughed. "Don't worry. Noah and I hunted last year and it was pretty pitiful. We didn't have a clue what we were doing and most of the time we spent wading from place to place trying to figure out how to get the ducks to come close enough to shoot. We'd pick a spot to hunt and then stand there and watch the ducks fly everywhere but where we were. Then we'd decide to move and wade through all the mud and grass to another spot where we'd seen ducks flying and once we got there we'd see ducks flying over the place we'd just come from. It was pretty frustrating. We're pretty green too, so we'll all learn together."

The sky in the east was just beginning to turn to a deep blue as we pulled up to the marsh side of the blind. Noah cut the motor and we coasted to a stop. "Let's get the decoys. We can get them out of the bags and unwind the cords," I said.

Noah stayed in the boat and Julio and I went up and got the decoys from the blind. We carried them back to the boat.

Julio dumped one sack out on the bottom of the boat and he

and I got the strings loose from the necks of the decoys while Noah pushed with an oar toward the edge of the pond on the backside of the island. Julio and I began sitting decoys out as we moved slowly through the shallow water and lily pads. Once we had the teal decoys out we put some mallards and a few wood ducks out and then Noah pushed us toward the island. We maneuvered the boat up to the island and tied a rope from the bow and stern to a couple of trees. As soon as we got tied up the dogs jumped out onto the island and took off sniffing. We picked up our guns and lunch and headed up the island to the blind.

When we got to the bridge Noah went across and waddled through the door. Then Julio and I went into the blind. The interior was pretty dark and we unlocked the top trap door and laid it back open. The open roof gave us a more light and a place to stand up straight.

"Looks good eh?" Noah said grinning.

I nodded. "The decoys look just like real ducks swimming around over there too."

He nodded and whistled softly for the dogs. A minute later Kate came huffing across the bridge and a little while after, Karen came across too. "Karen is a bit slower," Noah said grinning. "It takes a lot of steps with those little short legs to keep up to Kate."

Julio was scratching the dog's ears and grinned at me. "So does Karen think she's a retriever?"

I shrugged my shoulders. "She thinks she's a golden I guess. Last year we took her along and she'd crawl up on a muskrat house and watch us. We really didn't shoot many ducks for them to retrieve so I don't know if she'll try to fetch one or not. I guess we'll see if we get a duck."

The sky was brightening and the marsh began to take form. We could hear red winged black birds begin to sing their songs and soon we heard a hen mallard off in the distance calling. "Listen, that sounds just like what Harry taught us," I said.

"Call back and see if she answers," Noah said.

I dug my call out of my pocket and put it in my mouth and made a hail call as best I could. A few seconds later the hen called back to me. "Holy crap, she answered you!" Noah said excitedly.

"Call again."

I called another hail call and the hen called right back. We all giggled a little and I called again. She answered me. Then I called once more and we heard her call and then heard "quack, quack, quack."

"She's flying over here!" I said.

"Oh no, we don't have our guns loaded!" Julio said grabbing for his gun.

We all were trying to untie our gun cases and load up when the hen landed right in the middle of our decoys. We all dropped down below sight and tried to load up without shooting each other. I had a shell in my gun and closed the breech when I heard a splash. I peeked up over the side of the blind and there was Karen swimming toward the mallard.

"Oh no!"

Karen looked like a big muskrat swimming full throttle at the duck. The hen sat there and wagged her tail back and forth a couple of times and then sprang into the air and flew off into the marsh. We all stood up and looked as Karen sniffed the water where the duck had been.

"Well I guess we know now that she'll retrieve a duck," Noah said. "All we have to do is get her to wait until we shoot it first."

We all began laughing. Our duck hunt wasn't starting off to well but it was pretty funny. We called Karen back and when she got to the island she waddled up onto dry ground, shook herself off and came trotting across the bridge into the blind. She stood there looking at us as if to say, "Why didn't you guys shoot that one?"

Maybe we should block off the dog door," I said. "Just in case?"

"Good idea," Julio said.

We sat the food bag in front of the dog door leaving enough of it open so the dogs could look out and see any ducks we might drop and finished loading our guns. Julio had his single shot 16 gauge, Noah had a double barrel 12 gauge and I had a pump 12 gauge. I was allowed 3 shells in the gun so I had more shooting chances than the two of them. The sky was beginning to look blue and we heard a few shots far off in the marsh.

Noah grabbed the three stools and we situated them in the open front part of the blind. When we sat down on the stools our heads were just above the top rail on the front of the blind. We could see but were pretty hidden. The grass mat on the front of the blind was irregular and in places it stood above the blind wall so it was hard to see us sitting there on our stools. Hopefully, if a duck came, we would see it and be able to stand up and shoot it. At least that was the plan.

CHAPTER 24

THE SOUNDS OF GUNSHOTS began to increase as the sky got lighter. We'd hear a few shots and then watch and often would see some ducks flying in the general area where the shots had come from. Soon there was sporadic shooting all across the marsh.

"Sounds like there must be some ducks around," Julio said.

"Yeah it does," I said, "I just hope they don't all get shot before some come past us."

"Try calling again," Noah urged.

I put the call in my mouth and called. We watched the sky and saw nothing but a bunch of blackbirds and a crow flying out over the marsh. I called again.

Suddenly out of the corner of my eye I saw movement. I turned my head and saw seven little ducks just barely over the marsh grass going over our decoys.

"Crap! Look there, some came past and we didn't see them!"

"I was looking up in the sky," Noah said.

"So was I," Julio said. "What the heck were those?"

"I think Harry said that teal fly low over the grass and fly really fast," I said.

"He wasn't kidding was he?"

I shook my head. "I think we better get more advice from Harry when we can or we're going to be doing a lot of sitting and not much shooting."

It wasn't long and Julio spotted some ducks coming from the south of us. "Look they're coming right over us," he whispered.

We all turned and crouched down and five big ducks flew over

98

us about twenty yards high. They were just a little too far out over the marsh though. "Call them!" Noah said excitedly.

I made a hail call and they turned and swung back toward the decoys. "Holy smokes, they're coming!" Julio said.

The ducks came around and looked at our decoys and then started to land in with them. One brown duck changed her mind at the last minute and they all followed her up into the sky again. "Call!" Noah urged.

I called again and they turned. "Make the feeding call!"

I began to chuckle on the call and one of the ducks in the sky began to do the same call. "Oh my gosh, they're answering you," Julio said in a whisper.

The ducks swung around again and set their wings to land. Their orange feet came down and they began to glide down to the water.

"Let's shoot!" I said.

We all stood up and pulled our guns to our shoulders. The ducks saw us and began to flap wildly to get out of there. Kate began to bark and pushed the food bag down and jumped into the river. Karen went right after her.

I looked down the barrel of my gun and all I could see was ducks so I pulled the trigger thinking I couldn't miss. Julio shot his one shot and Noah shot one barrel and then the other. I pumped the empty shell out of my gun and shot again at the now rapidly rising ducks. Nothing fell so I pumped that empty shell out and shot the last one at the now departing ducks.

I lowered my gun and looked around. The two dogs were swimming around in the decoys and smoke was curling out of the end of Noah's double barrel. There was no sign of a duck anywhere.

"We missed?" I said.

Noah grinned. "Oops, that wasn't so good was it?"

Julio just shook his head. "I can't believe we missed them. They were right there."

"Kate, Karen, come on," I yelled. "Come on you two

knuckleheads."

"How the heck did we miss?" I said. "The sky was full of ducks I thought we'd drop every one of them."

Noah and Julio cracked open their guns and pulled the dead shells out and put in new ones. I fed three shells into the magazine of my gun and then jacked one into the chamber. The dogs arrived, crossed the bridge and then shook off when they got into the blind. "Oh yeah, that makes it perfect," Noah said laughing as mud and water dripped off his face.

We all had a good laugh and then set about figuring out a way to keep the dogs from stampeding the next time we had ducks come in. We wanted them to see the ducks so they knew where to look when and if we ever shot one but we also wanted them to wait for us to tell them to go. We finally came up with a half door that Kate couldn't push over.

Just as we were finishing the door Julio said, "Dang!"

I looked up at him. He shook his head. "There was a duck sitting in the decoys. When I stood up it got up and flew away."

Noah and I just laughed and we all sat down on our stools. Noah watched toward the marsh, I watched upriver and Julio watched downriver. We still heard a shot or two now and then but there was less shooting as the morning went on. We had another flock of ducks that we thought were mallards look at our decoys but they weren't interested in stopping and kept right on flying past.

After a while we all began to get hungry so we broke out our lunch bag and ate some sandwiches. "At least we won't starve," I said.

By about ten o'clock the shooting stopped all together. We sat there and watched the sky and saw nothing. "Where did they all go?" I said.

"They must have left from the whole marsh, nobody's shooting," Julio said.

We were kind of half dozing when I heard a thump. I looked over the side of the blind and there was Harry rowing his little boat across the pond where our decoys were sitting. Old Bea was sitting in the front with a grin on her face.

"Hey Harry, how you doin'" I said.

"Not bad boys, how did your morning go?"

"We got some shooting but no ducks, how about you?"

Harry coasted to a stop below the blind and held up a burlap sack. He took hold of the bottom and turned it over in the boat and a pile of ducks fell out. "I think I've got ten or eleven," he said.

Noah looked at me. "Shoot me will you?"

CHAPTER 25

HARRY PULLED UP to the island and we walked across the bridge and met him. Noah and I helped pull his boat up on the bank and he got out. Bea got out of the boat. Her coat was all wet and full of mud. She and our dogs took off galloping down the island.

"So you did get some shooting?" Harry asked.

"Well, yeah we shot our guns," I said.

Harry grinned. "And...?"

"We got zip Harry," Noah said. "We had some ducks come right in and we missed them all."

Harry burst out laughing. "Don't feel too bad boys, I've missed a few in my day too. Let me guess, you just shot into the flock thinking you couldn't miss."

We all nodded at once. "We shouldn't have done that I guess?" I said.

Harry smiled. "You've got to pick one duck out and concentrate on that one duck. You can't flock shoot. New hunters make that mistake all the time. They think there are so many ducks, how can you miss?"

"You're right Harry that's exactly what we did."

"Easy to correct," he said. "What kind were they?"

I told Harry we were sure they were mallards and he nodded that we were probably right.

"The bigger the duck the easier it is to make the mistake of not leading them boys," Harry said. "When you pick your duck you try to get your front bead right on his nose and then swing past him and pull the trigger as you go past. If they're just flying past you have to lead them farther than if they're landing. Smaller ducks like those teal look like they're going faster but they're really not that much faster. They look like they are because they're so small. Wait until you see some geese. They look like they're standing still but they're really moving."

We all were listening intently as Harry gave us pointers. Then we went on to tell Harry about our hunting mistakes for the morning and he listened and giggled a few times.

"I didn't know those teal could fly so fast," Julio said. "They came past like bullets."

"They're not going to hover over the decoys and hold up their wings and give up Julio," Harry said laughing.

I looked down into his boat. "You sure did good did you miss any?"

"I missed a few shots, but had a pretty good eye today. Do you guys know what these are?"

He held up a mallard and we all knew right away what it was. The he held up a gray mottled duck and another that looked just like it. "Those are both hen mallards," I said.

Harry shook his head. "I knew you'd say that. Look at their feet and bills. This one is a mallard. She has orange feet and an orange bill. But this one, her feet and bill are gray."

None of us had a clue. "It's a gadwall. They're not real common here but remember I said you have to look careful at the hens, they all look alike except for bill color, foot color and sometimes a wing patch."

He held up a wood duck and we knew it right away from its bright gaudy plumage. Then he held up two little ducks. Both were teal but one had a green patch on its wing and the other a blue patch. We figured those out too.

"See you guys learned something today even if you haven't gotten any ducks yet."

"You think they'll come back later?" I asked.

Harry nodded. "They're all out feeding. The mallards and teal will go to corn fields or soybean fields and feed. The wood ducks will fly up into the hills and land in streams and feed on acorns. Then about noon or so they'll come back and land in some pond to rest for the day. Late in the afternoon they'll fly out again for the evening feeding time. If you're patient you still have plenty of time to get some birds."

Well, that made us feel better. "Bea and I are heading home. I've got enough ducks for today and Bea is ready for her nap."

Harry called Bea and the dog jumped into the boat and sat wagging her tail. She was an old dog but she seemed like she loved to hunt and was ready for more. Harry got in and we pushed him off. "Don't give up boys, just remember pick out a target when they come in and be sure to lead them a bit. They're moving faster than you think."

We called the dogs and went back to the blind. We were getting hungry again so we broke out the lunch bag and sat eating and chatting. After a while Noah leaned back against the side of the blind and pulled his cap down over his eyes. "Time for a siesta, wake me if some ducks come."

Julio and I sat and talked quietly and kept a watch on the sky. He was telling me about how angry Marco had been when the pail of paint had slammed into him when Kate's tail began thumping against the side of the blind. I looked down and she was peeking through the dog door and whining. I looked up and there were six mallards sitting in the middle of our decoys. "Holy smokes, where did those come from?" I whispered.

I shook Noah and he woke up and looked around like he didn't know where he was. "What?" he said.

"Six mallards are sitting in the decoys," I whispered.

"Where'd they come from?"

"No clue, but they're there now, let's get ready and then jump up and get them."

We all had our guns already loaded so we all got ready and stood up. When the ducks saw us they all jumped into the air and what had been a peaceful little pond turned into chaos.

I put my front sight on the head of a drake and pulled the trigger. The gun roared and the duck dropped from the sky. I turned to look for another and just then Noah's gun went off and the hen I was aiming at dropped. Julio's gun barked and I heard him cuss. I looked for another target but by now the ducks were getting pretty high up in the air and out away from us. Noah shot one more time but missed. Julio snapped his single shot closed and cussed again. "Dang gun!"

When the smoke had cleared we looked and there were two dead ducks on the pond. Kate was going nuts trying to get out, so we opened the dog door and out she went followed by Karen. The two dogs swam over to the ducks and Kate grabbed the drake in her mouth and began swimming back to us. Karen was too small to hold the hen in her mouth so she took hold of one of the wings and began to tow the bird back.

We were all talking at once and laughing about the shooting when I noticed one of the decoys looked funny. "What happened to that decoy?" I asked.

Noah looked and began laughing. "It's got no head... somebody shot its head off."

"Wasn't me," I said. "I only shot once at the drake."

"I shot the hen with my first shot and my last shot was when they were up in the air a long way," Noah said.

Julio looked like he wanted to run away. "You guys gotta promise you won't tell Marco, I'd never hear the end of it. Every duck I aimed at seemed to drop from the sky just before I shot. Then I saw one that I thought hadn't taken off yet and...jeez I blew its head off and it was a decoy."

We laughed and promised him we'd keep his secret. "We'll have to tell Harry though," I said.

"Oh great...can't we just leave the decoy in the marsh someplace and say we lost it?"

Kate came across the bridge carrying her duck as proud as could be. Karen was still on the bank of the island dragging the hen by the wing. "I'll go help her," Julio said.

He took the duck from little Karen and she trotted alongside him very proud of herself.

"Well, we know that it can be done now I guess," I said. "Next time Julio gets the first shot."

Julio grinned.

CHAPTER 26

DUCKS CAME PAST later in the afternoon and we managed to scare away several of them. The shooting out across the marsh kept up until it started to get dark. Then everyone stopped shooting. As the sun set there were small flocks of ducks crossing the marsh to their evening roosting ponds but none came to us.

"I'll take the boat out and grab the decoys," Noah said.

"Let me go and I'll sit in front and pick up the decoys while you row," Julio said.

"I'll get things put away here and meet you on the bank."

The dogs went with Noah and Julio and I unloaded the guns and put the blind in order. I shut the roof down and locked it from the inside and then carried the guns and our empty lunch bag and our two ducks across the bridge. I went back and locked the blind door and picked up what was left and carried it off to the boat. Noah and Julio were waiting for me on the bank.

Julio helped me load the stuff and then he and I got in and we headed off for the fish market with the sky turning a dark blue. By the time we got to the shore it was pretty dark but Noah knew each turn so we had no problem getting home.

We unloaded the gear and Noah picked up the two ducks and we walked up to the market. Steffen was sitting talking to a customer when we walked in with our ducks. He grinned. "So the duck hunters return."

Noah nodded. "I hope you didn't have your appetite set for a big duck dinner," he said holding up the two ducks.

"That's it?" Steffen asked.

We nodded. "Ducks are harder to get than we thought," I said.

Steffen laughed. "I used to hunt ducks myself. I know what you're saying. It'll get easier as you have more practice. But then when you think you've got it all figured out, the ducks will make you look like fools again."

We nodded. We were sure of that.

"I'm going to sleep over at Sebastian's tonight," Noah said.

He went in the house and came back with a change of clothes and we all walked up to my house. Gram was waiting for us.

"I have the oven all heated up ready to roast ducks," she said with an impish grin.

"I hope you have a small guest list," I said.

She broke out laughing. "Well, just in case I roasted a couple of chickens."

Gram looked our ducks over and was impressed with the quality if not the quantity. "Those look nice and fat, I'll pluck them after supper and we can have roast duck tomorrow evening," she said.

That was fine with us since none of us had ever plucked a duck. We went upstairs and all took turns washing up and when we came down Gram had supper on the table. Even though we'd eaten well in the blind we dug in like we hadn't eaten in a week.

Just as we were finishing supper the phone rang. It was my Dad. Gram talked for a minute and then handed it to me.

"Hey Dad, how's it going?" I said.

"Things are fine I was hoping to talk to your mother."

"She's working an extra shift today. Somebody called in sick. Are you coming home soon?"

"With the weather so nice we're taking on extra trips yet. Right now we have our last trip scheduled for the first part of November. We'll leave Chicago on the 10th and sail to Quebec and get there on the 12th. That should be the last trip of the year. So I'll be home for deer hunting."

"Great, I'm looking forward to that. We've been duck hunting more this year and it's a lot of fun." I told him about our blind and our first hunt today and he laughed when I described our errors.

"Duck hunting is one thing that can make a man very humble," he said.

We talked a bit about duck hunting and then he hung up.

"Where is your dad working?" Julio asked.

"He works on freighter on Lake Michigan, it's called the *Novadoc*. He's the engineer."

"It must be hard for him to be gone so much."

"It is but he makes really good money so I guess it's worth it. He has a lot of time off in the winter though."

The phone rang again and I picked it up thinking it was Dad again. "This is Harry, I was just wondering if you guys got any more ducks?"

I turned to the other guys. "It's Harry," I said. "Well Harry, some mallards must have walked through the marsh and swam out into our pond because we didn't see them fly in, but we did manage to bag two of them when we saw them swimming around in the decoys."

I could hear Harry giggling. "How about I meet you guys at your duck blind tomorrow at dawn and maybe I can help you a bit?"

"Really? You'd do that Harry?" I said.

"Sure, I'd like to hunt from a luxury hotel like that and Bea would too."

"We'll be there Harry. Don't worry we'll bring plenty of food and some coffee for you too."

We said goodbye and then I passed the news on to the other guys. "Maybe we'll actually get a duck or two tomorrow," Julio said grinning.

I hoped we didn't completely make fools of ourselves with our poor shooting, but it would be good to see how a pro did it.

CHAPTER 27

JULIO STAYED AT MY HOUSE again and the three of us were up long before dawn. We ate some cereal for breakfast and loaded up the sandwiches Gram had made for us the night before. We took a thermos of coffee and one of hot chocolate with us too.

Once we were all loaded into the boat we started down the backwater cuts toward the blind. As usual Noah knew right where to turn and in about fifteen minutes we pulled up to the island. Harry's little duck boat was already pulled up on the shore.

"Well I thought you guys might have overslept," Harry said. He was sitting on a log on the island with Bea lying at his feet.

"No way Harry," I said.

We gathered up our gear and Noah took the key and unlocked the blind door. We all crowded inside. With four of us and three dogs it was a bit cramped but we didn't worry about it. Harry had brought a little folding stool with him so we all had a seat. I noticed Harry was carrying three guns.

"You think you got enough artillery Harry?" I asked.

The old man grinned. "I brought some extra," he said. First he uncased a pump gun and handed it to Julio. "Here, you try this one. That little single shot doesn't give you much of a chance at hitting a duck."

"Wow, thanks Harry," Julio said looking over the gun.

"I have lots of guns. Here I brought a couple of extra boxes of 12 gauge shells for you too."

Julio stood his own gun in the corner and loaded up the new pump gun. I loaded my gun and so did Noah. Harry pulled another pump gun out of the next gun case and loaded it and stood it in the corner. Then he uncased a very long gun from the last case.

"Holy cow, what is that?" I said.

Harry laughed. "This, my boy, is a double barrel 10 gauge. It shoots a 3½ inch magnum shell that will drop a duck at 60 yards."

We were all in awe of the huge gun. The thing must have been over 5 feet long. Harry tripped a lever and the thing gun clicked open. He reached into his pocket and pulled out the biggest shotgun shells I'd ever seen. He dropped the two shells into the breech and they made a sound like "Kathunk!"

"What the heck are we going to shoot that at?" Noah said.

"We might not shoot it at all," Harry said. "But I've been seeing a few flocks of geese this fall and I thought if some happened to come past here, it'd be fun to see you guys take a poke at one of them with that gun."

"I'll shoot it," Julio said quickly.

Harry looked him up and down. "No offense Julio but you might be a bit scrawny to handle it. I don't know if you're man enough to shoot that gun."

Julio kind of bristled up. "I'm tougher than you think Harry."

Harry nodded. "We'll see. The geese might not even come past. Noah, let's get the decoys out," he said.

Harry and Noah took the boat out and Harry stood in the bow and tossed out decoys and directed Noah where to go. When they got done the pond looked like a little pond full of duck families. Harry had arranged them into family size groups and left a 'landing hole' near the blind.

I looked at Julio. "Already we learned something."

He nodded. When Harry and Noah came back we called the dogs and once they were in the blind we closed up the door and settled down. It would be fifteen or twenty minutes until dawn so we had time to get everything situated.

"I think with 4 of us shooting it would be best if we took turns," Harry said.

We all agreed and decided that Julio and I would shoot first and then Harry and Noah would shoot at the next ducks. Harry took out his duck call and made a few quiet quacks. "Why don't you do a hail call?" I asked.

"There's no one to hail to," Harry said. "I'm just making a hen mallard call that sounds like she's just puttering around and all is well. If we see some ducks in the air, we'll hail them."

That made sense. We'd learned another thing.

The sky turned gray and then a deep blue and we heard wings overhead. "Probably wood ducks," Harry said. "They get up early and head to the woods for acorns."

A bit later Harry put his call in his mouth and did a little more excited quack. Then he did a hail call."

I looked at the sky and way off up river I saw about a dozen ducks crossing the marsh. Harry called again and they turned our way.

"Holy smokes, they're coming," I said.

"Get ready you two," Harry whispered.

Julio and I got our guns ready and Harry called again. The flock of ducks turned and circled right over our pond. "When they come around again, take them," Harry whispered.

He did a little feeding call and the ducks spun and set their wings and began to drop toward the water. "Now!" Harry said.

Julio and I stood up and the ducks saw us. They were dropping and had to flap like mad to get going upward again and for a couple of seconds they were nearly motionless in the air. I picked out a drake mallard and put my bead right on his beak. I pulled the trigger and he dropped like a rock. Julio did the same just to the right of my duck and another drake dropped. By now the rest were gaining altitude and I picked the closest duck which was a hen and dropped her too. Julio shot two more times but missed.

"Nice shooting," Harry said, his eyes twinkling. "Bea, fetch," he said.

I opened the dog door and the three dogs piled out and down the dog bridge into the water. Bea swam up to a drake, grabbed it in her mouth and turned back to the blind. Kate grabbed the hen and little Karen grabbed the other drake's head and began to tow it back.

Harry broke out laughing. "That little dog has lots of sprit doesn't she?"

"She thinks she's a Labrador," Noah said watching his little friend proudly. "I hope we don't get a goose or she'll try that too."

The dogs came back and Bea and Kate brought their ducks into the blind. Noah went down to the shore and helped Karen with her duck. When they were all in the blind again we shut the door and looked at our ducks.

"Not bad shooting," Harry said.

"It helps to have the ducks fooled enough to try to land," I said.

"It all comes with practice boys," Harry said. "And the practicing is always a lot of fun."

We all sat down again and soon Harry nodded toward the shore. "There's a small bunch of teal just over the grass," he said.

We all looked and I could see the little ducks flying like bullets just above the top of the tall grass. "They'll come and look at us," Harry said. "Get ready Noah."

Harry and Noah moved into shooting position and a few seconds later the half dozen teal came buzzing over our pond. The two of them stood up and began shooting. Harry shot twice and two teal dropped. Noah shot all three shells and got one on his last shot." The dogs took off for the pond.

"Jeez, those things are quick," Noah said shaking his head.

"They don't give you much time to decide which one you want to shoot at," Harry said giggling. "You did ok. I got lucky by getting two."

We all knew better but it was nice of Harry not to brag. The dogs came back with the ducks and Karen was carrying her own this time. Teal were more her size.

For the next hour ducks came past. Some were enticed to visit us, some were not interested. When the action slowed we had 9 ducks piled up in the back of the blind. "Not a bad morning,"

Harry said. "They'll be out feeding for a while and then we'll get some more action when they come back to rest for the day."

"Wow Harry that was fantastic," I said. "I sure learned a lot today."

"I'm glad Sebastian, but like I said, learning and practice is lots of fun too."

We all agreed on that for sure. We broke out some coffee and chocolate and had a sandwich. Harry was telling us about a day he'd had last fall when he'd gotten 17 ducks in just over an hour. "It seemed that every time I pulled the trigger... listen!"

We all strained our ears. Then I heard it. "Geese?"

Harry nodded.

CHAPTER 28

"**GET READY,**" Harry whispered. "They're coming right down the marsh."

I peeked up over the front of the blind and saw a string of geese floating lazily down the river. They were moving really slow and weren't very high.

"I'll see if I can get them to look us over," Harry said reaching inside his jacket and pulling out a long call. He put the call to his lips and blew a single "honk" on it. Then he blew two more. The geese began to drift our way.

"Can you call them in?" Julio asked excitedly.

"No we don't have any goose decoys out there but they'll hear that lone call and come past. They think there must be a lost friend down there and they'll come over and look. If we're lucky they might come in range."

We were all pretty excited and got our guns up in shooting position. Harry reached back and grabbed the 10 gauge. "Here one of you can shoot this. It'll kick pretty hard so be ready."

Noah turned to take the gun from Harry's hand and Julio grabbed it grinning. "I haven't shot as many ducks as you guys, let me try it ok?"

Noah nodded. "You got it," he said.

Harry called again and the geese came closer. "When they get past the weeds on the outside of the pond they'll be in range. Don't let their size fool you. They're moving faster than you think. Be sure to lead them."

"How far Harry?"

"At least six feet."

I looked at Noah and he frowned. Six feet? Jeez that was a long way to lead a bird. Maybe Harry was messing with us.

"Get ready," Harry said.

The geese passed over the decoys and one of them called

down to the lost goose. The three of us stood up and began shooting. I picked out a goose and shot and the second goose behind him started flying like it was hit. I aimed for that one and then remembered to lead and shot again. The goose dropped to the marsh. Noah missed his first shot and then connected with a goose on his second.

Julio hoisted the big goose cannon to his shoulder and aimed at the lead goose. It was coming closer and closer and getting right up over the top of the blind when he pulled the trigger. The blast from the gun actually shook the blind. Karen let out a whoop and climbed under a stool. It sounded like a bomb had gone off. My ears began to ring from the loud blast. Julio's shoulder was slammed back so hard he lost his balance and fell over backwards over his stool. The goose flew on.

When the smoke cleared Harry was laughing so hard he had to sit down. Julio was sitting on the floor with a bewildered look on his face. There was smoke curling up from both barrels of the 10 gauge. "Holy smokes that thing is a cannon!" he said.

Kate and Bea ran down the dog bridge to get the birds we'd shot but Karen was still a little shaken from the 10 gauge going off. Noah picked her up and cuddled her. "It's ok little girl," he said.

Harry was wiping his eyes and shaking his head. "You're not suppose to shoot both barrels at once Julio. But that was a good try, want to use the gun some more?"

Julio grinned. "You can have it back Harry I'll stick with my little gun from now on." He massaged his shoulder and shook his head. "Wow!" he said.

"Why'd you shoot both barrels?" I said laughing.

"I didn't know which one to shoot first so I just pulled both triggers at once. I guess that's not how to do it," Julio said grinning.

Harry was wiping tears from his eyes. "Oh that's one to add to my duck stories."

"I'd better take the boat and help the dogs," Noah said. "They both look like they're having trouble with that big of a bird."

I looked over the blind and saw Kate towing her goose through the water and Bea was trying to swim with her goose in her mouth but not making much headway. Noah went out and helped them and then they both swam to shore while Noah put the boat away. He came into the blind carrying the two geese by the neck.

"Dang these things are huge," he said hoisting up the two big birds.

I looked them over and they were really impressive. "Wow, now that's a real bird."

"I noticed you let the lead goose go and shot one back in the string," Harry said with a twinkle in his eye.

"Would you believe I wanted that other goose?" I said.

He shook his head.

"You were right as usual Harry. I was aiming at the first goose but I guess they do move faster than I thought."

"As long as you learn from your mistake its ok," he said.

We hunted the rest of the afternoon but the action wasn't real fast. The sky was bright and high and the ducks were late coming back from their afternoon feed so we didn't have any come in at dusk to roost on our pond. Harry declared it was time to stop shooting so we packed up and loaded the boat. Noah went slowly through the pond and we picked up the decoys and then headed back to the landing. We towed Harry's boat behind us and he rode with us to the channel that would lead him upriver to his place.

On the way Harry motioned to a lone tree out in the marsh about a quarter of a mile away. "See that little lone tree?" he asked.

I nodded.

"That's where I hunt. It's a tiny little island but high enough that it's dry and sound. There's a little pond right next to it. I just sit in the tall grass under the tree. I've been hunting there for over 30 years, ever since I moved here."

"Must be a good place," I said.

He nodded. "It's kind of between two bigger ponds so the ducks make a lot of trips back and forth. There's plenty of action for Bea and me."

When we got to the channel we pulled up on the shore and Harry and Bea got out. We untied his boat and he got in. We thanked Harry for all the help and lessons. Julio handed him the gun he'd borrowed but Harry told him to keep it for the season. "Just wipe it down every night so it doesn't rust," he said.

The three of us motored back to the fish market and unloaded all the gear and ducks and the two geese. Julio called his dad and while we waited I turned and smiled at my two friends. "A pretty good day hey?"

Noah nodded. "Not bad for a bunch of rookies. That Harry what a guy. I wonder how old he is?"

"I don't know. He's talked about things back seventy years or more ago. I'd guess he's probably around 80. I'll ask Gram. She knows everyone and everything."

When Julio's dad pulled into the parking lot I told Julio to take all the birds with him. "Tell them you got them all," I said.

Julio grinned. "I was planning on telling them that all along," he said with a goofy smile. "Hey guys, thanks for letting me hunt with you. I've had a blast so far and we're just getting started. I really appreciate it."

"Hey, I'm glad we got to know you and how things have turned out," Noah said. "Now if your stubborn brother would get his head out of his butt we might even get to be friends with him."

Julio put the birds in the trunk of his dad's car and waved. "See you in school tomorrow," he said and off they went.

I said goodbye to Noah and Kate and I hiked up the hill toward my house. We had school the next five days so there wouldn't be much time to hunt. But next weekend we'd give'm heck again."

CHAPTER 29

THE NEXT DAY AT SCHOOL Julio came trotting down the hall with a huge grin on his face. He walked up to us. "You should have seen my family when I came home with all those ducks and those two geese. Geez, they think I'm the great white hunter now."

We grinned at our new buddy. "What did Marco have to say?" I asked.

Julio laughed. "He came home with two little teal and just about pooped when he saw my ducks. He was just about to explode," he said.

We all had a good laugh and then stopped as Marco walked past giving us a "death stare". "Ooooh I'm scared," Noah laughed.

Marco stopped and was going to say something but thought better of it and moved on.

The week passed slowly and the weather continued to be beautiful. It was now the late part of October and we hadn't had one night where it got cool enough to frost and kill the gardens and flowers. Gram was still harvesting fresh tomatoes from our garden and everyone was marveling at how great a fall it had been.

Friday after school we walked down to Harry's cabin and talked to him for a while. We invited him to hunt with us again but he said he'd just go to his little island. "That's a three person blind," he said. "It's a little crowded with me and an extra dog. You guys know what you're doing now. Bea and I will hunt on our little pond."

Julio and Noah stayed over at my house again and we set out in the dark for the blind. Noah's dad needed the big boat for fishing for the day so we all piled into the little boat. It was a little crowded but not too bad. We'd left the decoys and all the extra gear in the blind since we could lock it up and all we had were the dogs and our guns and lunch.

When we got to the blind, Julio went with Noah to set out the decoys and I took the dogs up to the blind. I unlocked the door and opened the roof and got things ready and by the time I was finished they walked across the bridge. We all loaded our guns and stood them against the side of the blind and sat down to wait for dawn.

"So is your moron brother hunting today?" Noah asked Julio.

"He was kind of smug about it but yeah, he said he'd be out and bet me he'd have more ducks than I would by the end of the day."

"What's he going to do?" I said. "Buy some?"

We laughed and then sat and watched the morning come. Soon the blackbirds began to sing and the sounds of the marsh increased. It was still pretty dark when we heard the whistling of duck wings overhead. "Probably some woodies heading to the hills," I said quietly.

A little while later Julio whispered, "Look up river, there's some big ducks, maybe mallards."

We strained our eyes into the sky and soon could see about half a dozen ducks coming our way. They were out over the marsh headed right toward us. "They're a little too high," I said.

The words had barely left my lips when someone up the marsh about three hundred yards shot twice at the ducks. They flew up higher and headed off toward the river bank too far off course for us. "What an idiot, those ducks were way too high," Noah said.

We shook our heads. It wasn't long and a pair of ducks came following pretty much the same path as the last ones had. When they got to about the same place there was one shot and they flew higher and on they went, much too high for us to shoot.

"They're following the ponds that are out there," Noah said.

"Somebody's hunting right in the path the ducks take to get to us."

"I wouldn't care if they'd shoot at ducks in range but those are too high," I said.

The rest of the morning the same thing happened every time we saw ducks coming from the north. They'd be right on course to come over our decoys and the hunter up river from us would shoot and scare them off. We got a little shooting from ducks coming up river from below us but very little.

About noon we heard the unmistakable honk of geese and looked to see a nice flock coming down the marsh. "Oh no they're going to right over that bonehead," Noah said.

Sure enough when the geese got to where the hunter was sitting they were much too high but he shot at them anyway and they went even higher. We watched them fly past us.

"That's it!" Noah said.

"That's what?"

"I'm going over there."

"Noah we don't own the marsh, that guy has a right to hunt there as much as we do," I said.

"Yeah, but I'd bet he's just shooting at those ducks to keep them from us."

"You don't suppose it's..." Julio said.

"That's exactly what I think," Noah said. "I'm going to see if he'll agree to stop shooting at the ducks that are too high for him."

Noah set his gun against the side of the blind and opened the door. He was wearing his hip boots and walked across the bridge to the boat and then got in and started up the motor. "I'll be back in a bit," he said as he motored out into the channel and then started up the river.

Julio and I watched Noah go upriver for a way and then turn into the marsh. We heard the motor shut off and then it was quiet. I looked over at Julio. He grinned.

"There're some ducks coming," I said.

We watched as three small ducks began flying down the marsh. When they got to the right area the hunter shot once at them and they flew off toward the river. We couldn't see or hear anything but after about half an hour Noah came back down the channel in the boat. He pulled up on the shore and got out and came to the blind.

"Well?" I asked.

Noah grinned. "I had a little talk with the guy who was shooting at all the ducks and convinced him it was in his best interest not to do that any more."

"Who was it?" Julio asked.

"Someone from town who asked not to be identified," Noah said with a smirk on his face.

"Was it Marco?" Julio asked.

"Let's say it's someone close to you," Noah said. "Look there's some ducks coming."

A nice flock of big ducks that might have been mallards was coming down the marsh and they flew right over the spot where the person had been shooting. There wasn't a sound. They flew on toward us and I called to them. They were mallards and a couple set their wings and began to drop into the pond. Then one of the flock quacked and they followed the hen up and around the pond. They circled and I began to make a fairly decent sounding feeding call. They circled again and all set their wings and began to land. We stood up and began shooting and when the whole thing was over there were four mallards on the water.

"Holy smokes, that was good," I said excitedly. "I didn't think I could call them like that."

"You sounded just like Harry," Julio said laughing.

The dogs went out and brought in two ducks and then went back and got the second two. Noah helped Karen with hers since they were pretty big ducks.

I was pretty proud of my calling skills. It wasn't long and a small flock of what we thought were mallards came across the marsh and were headed toward the hills just a little way up from us. I pulled out my call and hailed them. They kept on flying as if they were all deaf. I called again and the same thing happened. I tried a feeding call and when that didn't work I tried a come back call. The ducks flew on.

"Well, there goes the idea that I can call any ducks we see," I said.

"Harry said sometimes they're headed someplace and they don't want to stop," Julio said. "Maybe those had something planned." I guess Harry was right as usual but I still felt a little disappointed that they'd ignored me like that. Maybe I wasn't the expert duck caller I thought I was.

We hunted the rest of the day and got shooting at several small bunches of ducks. The action wasn't as good as the weekend before but we had enough shooting to keep us happy.

When we got back home we had 9 ducks and Noah took them for his family. We decided to walk into town and then to Harry's cabin. On the way Harry came driving down the street toward my house. He stopped and parked and we talked over the day's hunt with him.

"We had a sky buster out there today," Harry said. "I hate those guys. They don't hit anything and even if they do all they managed to do is cripple the ducks so they go to waste."

"I went over and had a little talk with him," Noah said. "I don't think he'll sky bust anymore."

Harry grinned. "You persuaded him to be more restrained in his shooting?"

Noah nodded. "Oh yeah."

CHAPTER 30
_____

THE THREE OF US stopped at Harry's cabin the night before the next weekend which would be the first weekend in November. He's told us earlier that we should stop and pick up some diving duck decoys. They were late ducks and hadn't shown up at all yet so he figured they'd be coming one of these days.

Harry was in his shed sorting decoys when we walked up. "Hey, come in boys," he said. He had a couple of piles of decoys lying on the floor.

"You think the divers will be here this weekend Harry?" Noah asked.

"I don't know if it will be this weekend but they'll be coming soon. November starts Friday so it's got to be getting cold soon. The local ducks are nearly all gone south or have been shot so if we don't get some northern ducks soon our duck shooting will be pretty slim."

We'd already noticed that happening. The last couple of weekends there'd been fewer and fewer ducks and much less shooting across the marsh. Our duck harvest had dropped to only a couple of ducks per day too.

"I've got two strings for you," Harry said. He picked up a duck with a slate blue colored bill. "Can you guess what this is?"

"I'm no expert Harry," I said, "but if I had to guess I'd say it's a blue bill."

Harry grinned. "Very good, so what's its real name smart guy?"

"Umm," I said.

"Scaup," Julio volunteered.

"Ah somebody was listening I see," Harry said. "These are scaup or blue bills. They fly in a string and are dumb as rocks. Often if you shoot one from the flock as they pass by, the rest will turn around and go back to see where their buddy went. Sometimes they'll come back three or four times before they get the idea it's not a good place to be."

We all laughed at Harry's description of the ducks. "Not what you'd call geniuses," Noah said. Harry nodded.

"I've got them all in one string. The first one and the second one and the third have a weight on it and the last one too. What you need to do is string them out in a long line. Start at the bottom and as you work upriver, put that third decoy down and then take the first two and put them to the inside of the string, making a kind of a fish hook with them. Put the first two decoys closer to the land side and leave enough room for the real ducks to land between the decoys and the shore. Keep them on the river side of your blind. Blue bills will see them and fly over them and try to land inside the bend of the fish hook. That should get you some good pass shooting at them."

We all acknowledged that we knew what he was talking about. "And these are Canvasbacks, the king of ducks," Harry said holding up a large gray duck with a sloping forehead. They aren't as dumb as the blue bills but they'll come past and take a look at you. Put these six decoys in a little group up river from your blind on the river side inside of the blue bill decoys. The cans will swing past and look too."

We were pretty excited about having new ducks to shoot at. The pickings had been pretty slim for the last few days we'd hunted.

"There may be other ducks too," Harry said. "There's one

called a ring bill that is a cousin to the blue bill. Ring bills are pretty dumb too and will come in pretty easy. You might also see some medium size ducks that have a white wing patch. The male has a white head also. Those are widgeon. They're a puddle duck like the mallards and decoy to your mallard decoys. They're later ducks so we might see some of them now."

"Wow Harry, you sure know a lot about all this stuff," I said.

"Sebastian, I've been hunting for these birds for over 60 years, I guess I've learned a bit about it."

"Harry, do you mind, how old are you?" Julio said.

"I'm not ashamed of my age Julio. I'm 80. I've been tromping around in these marshes since I was about 14... a long time ago."

"That's amazing Harry," Noah said.

"I love the marsh. Not only hunting ducks but all the stuff you can see. I love to watch the muskrats building their houses for winter. I love to watch the beaver cutting trees and making dams. Once in a while you get lucky and see a mink or an otter and they're great fun to watch. I've seen eagles grab muskrats off their houses. I once saw a Peregrine Falcon catch a teal in mid-air. That's not something that many people have seen. Yes boys, I've spent a lot of time in this marsh. It wouldn't be a bad place to die when the time comes."

We couldn't imagine Harry dying. He was so full of life and loved the outdoors so much that we thought he'd go on forever. We thanked him for the decoys and then he offered to haul us and the decoys to the fish market. When we got there we unloaded them and he said he'd be listening for our shots in the morning. We watched as he drove out of the driveway in his old pickup.

"Dang, he's one of a kind isn't he?" Noah said.

"They don't make many of them like Harry," I said.

We stowed the decoys in the little boat and walked to my house for the night. We'd gotten into a habit of Julio and Noah staying over on the weekend and it worked out pretty well for our hunting and for our friendship.

Julio had turned out to be a lot like Noah and me. He loved the outdoors and was a lot of fun to be with.

After spending a while with Gram and Mom we went up and got undressed for bed. Julio took his cot as usual with Karen sleeping beside him and Noah and I got in my bed with Kate between us.

"Our duck season would have been pretty much crap if we hadn't met Harry," I said after I turned out the light.

"You can say that again," Noah said. "We'd probably have given up and gone squirrel hunting by now."

"I hate to say it," Julio said, "but I'm ready for some colder weather so we get some of those new northern ducks down here."

"I agree. I like the nice weather but we need some new ducks to shoot at. We can just hope the weather turns soon."

CHAPTER 31

GRAM WAS UP BEFORE WE WERE and had a big plate of scrambled eggs, bacon and a pile of toast ready for us when we came downstairs.

"Gram you don't have to get up and do this," I said. "We could eat some cereal and toast."

"You need a good breakfast, don't worry I've been feeding hunters for a long time. I'm usually up this early anyway. I fed your dad and his friends and my husband and his friends for many years. Besides, you guys would mess up my kitchen so I'd rather just get up and do it myself."

We began eating and in no time the food was gone. Gram had a sack of sandwiches ready for us and two thermos of chocolate. "You guys keep an eye on the sky," she said. "It's November now and the weather can turn real quickly."

"We will Gram," I said. We picked up the lunch and the three of us and the dogs walked down the road to the fish market where we loaded up and headed out into the marsh in the dark.

When we got to the blind I went up and grabbed our puddle duck decoys and tossed them into the boat and Noah and Julio went to set them and our new decoys out. I opened up the blind, loaded all the guns, got the stools situated and by the time I was finished they were pulling the boat up onto the shore on the island. They came into the blind and we called the dogs and settled in.

It was a warm morning and there was a stiff breeze coming from the west making our decoys "swim" around nicely. I looked at our new decoys on the river side of the blind, swimming along in the current. They looked pretty darn real to me. I hoped the ducks thought so too.

The sky brightened and soon the marsh birds were chirping and singing. We watched the sky for ducks. In another fifteen minutes the sky had turned bright blue and the sun was sneaking up the backside of the big bluffs to the east.

"Not much action today," Noah said.

"Not a shot anywhere," Julio said.

"Usually somebody does a little shooting right after dawn, but not one shot. I wonder if there are any ducks left around this part of the river?"

"Harry said they're getting scarce," Julio said. "You know if you think about it, we've probably shot nearly 50 ducks so far. If every other group of hunters did that too, it's a lot of ducks. We've probably shot most of the ducks that lived around here."

"You're right about that," I said. "But its November, the ducks that live in the north, and in Canada should be coming soon, it's got to be getting cold up there."

The morning sun was now shining down over the bluff and warmed up the blind. I noticed that Noah had leaned back against the side and was sleeping. I was just about asleep too when Julio poked me.

"Is that a duck?" he said pointing upriver.

I looked and nodded. "I think so it's flying like a duck."

We watched the lone duck come down along the edge of the marsh and then turn out to the east. It was getting close to Harry's little tree that we could see way over on the other side of the tall grass. We saw the duck flair up like it had seen something that frightened it and then it disappeared into the trees.

"I wonder if Harry saw it and just shooed it away," I said grinning.

"Or he might have not seen it until too late," he replied.

Morning became noon and we ate our lunch. By mid-afternoon we'd not seen any more ducks. "We should have brought our fishing poles," I lamented.

The others nodded. "We'll have to bring a deck of cards tomorrow and a cribbage board," Noah said. "Julio do you know how to play cribbage?"

Julio nodded. "Like a pro."

The sun was just disappearing into the skyline on the Minnesota side of the river when Noah and Julio put the boat into the water and began rowing around picking up the decoys. I put the blind in order and waited until they got back with the decoys. We stowed them in the blind and locked it up.

The dogs looked kind of confused. "I think they wonder why we didn't shoot anything," Noah said scratching Kate's ears.

"At least you didn't have to get wet today old girl," I said to her and she wagged her tail.

"Well time to head home. I bet we're not the only ones who are coming in empty today," I said.

When we got back to the fish market Harry's pickup was sitting by the dock. He was standing on the dock talking to Noah's dad.

"Got a lot of bullets left?" he asked us as we tied up.

"Never fired a shot, how about you?"

He grinned. "I should have shot that lone hen mallard that came over this morning but I didn't have the heart to do it. I think that's the last duck on the whole river."

Noah grinned at Harry. "We thought maybe you were asleep and didn't see it."

"I sleep with one eye open," the old man said.

"Well I'm not expecting a lot tomorrow," I said.

"They've got to come down soon," Harry said. "There are tens of thousands of ducks in Canada and northern Wisconsin and Minnesota that'll funnel right down the Mississippi. They'll come one of these days and then we'll have some amazing shooting."

"I hope you're right," I said.

"Don't worry, they'll come," he said. "Well, time for old Bea and me to get home and get some supper. Are you guys going out in the morning?"

"We've got nothing better to do," Julio said.

"That's the sprit," Harry said. He started his old pickup and rattled out of the parking lot.

Noah's dad watched his old friend drive away. "That's one old river rat, boys. If you guys learned half of what that old man knows about this river you'd be pretty dang smart."

"You're right about that Dad," Noah said. "I just hope he's right about all those ducks coming.

"I'd bet on it," his dad said.

CHAPTER 32

THE NEXT MORNING was Sunday and since the ducks were so scarce, we decided to get up later and go to church with Gram and Mom. They were very surprised when we told them of our intentions. We figured that if we went this weekend and the ducks came during the week, we'd be able to talk our way out of going next week when the hunting was better.

"Maybe you can pray and ask God to send you more ducks," Gram said with a sly smile.

After church we loaded up our lunch sack and took along a deck of cards and a cribbage board for the blind. On the way out through the channel we saw three little ducks flying out over the marsh. They were a long way from our blind so we didn't think we'd missed out on anything.

When we got to the blind we put out the decoys and then sat down and began to watch the sky. We heard a couple of shots far downriver from us a while later.

"Probably those three ducks flew past someone," Noah said.

We ate lunch and played cards and watched the sky. Late in the afternoon we saw a flock of big birds coming down the river right on the channel.

"Look, are those geese coming?" Julio said excitedly.

The big birds were flying in a straight line and not in a V like geese usually flew and they looked too dark, but we waited until they got closer. Then when they got close we decided that they were Cormorants.

"Those things eat fish," Julio said. "I've heard they're terrible to eat."

"We'll save our bullets," I said.

The string of Cormorants flew right past the blind and we were tempted to shoot a couple just for practice but we decided that killing them just for fun wasn't a good idea.

The day passed and we didn't fire a shot. At dusk we put the blind in order and went back home. It had been kind of a bad weekend for duck hunting.

The next day at school we talked to a few of our friends who also hunted and they reported the same results. There were no ducks in our part of the river.

We walked over to Harry's cabin after school Thursday and found Harry sitting on his dock fishing for bluegills. "Hey Harry, how they biting?" I asked as we walked onto the dock.

"Not much better than the ducks are flying," Harry said.

"You expect them soon?" Noah asked.

"They've got to come soon boys. This coming weekend is Armistice Day weekend. Monday is a holiday. I've never seen it that some northern ducks weren't in the area by Armistice Day. We can only hope I guess."

"We won't have school Monday so I suppose we'll hunt, though I'm getting kind of tired of sitting and playing cards," Julio said.

Harry laughed. "Don't give up yet. If you get there on the right day you'll have shooting like you've never seen before."

We sure hoped Harry was right.

When I got home Gram was canning tomatoes. "Something is going to happen," she said. "The squirrels are packing nuts away like there's no tomorrow. The blue jays have been pecking sunflower seeds out of the sunflower heads in the garden and flying off with their mouths full of them. The wooly bear caterpillars are crawling all over the place looking for the right spot to make their cocoons. Nature knows a change is coming."

"So you're going to clean out the garden?"

"I'm going to get everything I can from it before the weather changes. I feel like something bad is coming Sebastian. Are you and your friends going out on the river this weekend?"

"Yeah Gram, Harry says the ducks will be coming down from the north soon and we want to be there when they come."

"I don't like the idea of you guys out there. I think you should stay away until we see what's making the wildlife act so strange."

"Oh come on Gram, we've got a huge weather-tight blind and we know what we're doing. Don't worry about us."

"I don't know, I'm not going to be happy to see you guys out there," she said.

Just then the phone rang and it was my dad. "Hey I just wanted to tell you that we're going on our last trip of the season," he said.

"Great Dad," I said. "When will you be home?"

"We're leaving Chicago for Port Alfred, Quebec on Sunday. We should be there by Tuesday, unload and then we'll go to dry dock. I'll be home by the weekend. I'll call so somebody can come to La Crosse and pick me up at the train station."

"Great," I said. "We've been doing really well duck hunting. Well, at least until this weekend. Do you know Harry Gillette Dad?"

"Of course, everyone knows Harry," he said.

"Well he's been helping us with our duck hunting. He's really a quite a guy isn't he?"

"You can say that again. Harry is one of a kind. Maybe if I get back next week I can hunt with you guys and get together with Harry."

"That'd be great Dad I'll tell Harry you're coming home."

We talked a bit longer and then I hung up. I could hardly wait for the weekend now, and if some ducks got here I could show Dad our blind and all we'd learned from Harry.

CHAPTER 33

THE WEEK PASSED QUICKLY and the weather stayed warm and dry. Everyone was marveling at how warm it was and wondering if we were ever going to get some cooler weather. Gram worked feverishly harvesting everything she could from the garden. She was bound and determined that something bad was coming and she wanted to be ready.

We had several loads of firewood in the back yard that had been drying all summer and she coaxed Noah and Julio and me into splitting it and stacking it against the back of the house. We didn't mind and it got our thoughts off the upcoming weekend and how anxious we were to get some new ducks into the area so we'd have something to shoot at.

Our plan was for Julio to come over after school Friday and then the three of us would hunt all three days of the holiday weekend. Since we didn't have school on Monday we were hoping there would be some new ducks on the river to make the weekend a good one for hunting.

Friday evening we went over to Harry's for a fish fry. He'd

stopped and left word with Gram for us to come and eat with him so we all walked down to his cabin. We could smell some great aromas coming from his cabin as we walked up.

"Come on in boys," he said. "I've just about got everything ready."

'You must have had some better luck fishing," Julio said.

Harry grinned. "I had a pretty good day and thought rather than freeze the fish, why not eat them fresh. Sit, I've got it all ready, let's eat."

We sat at Harry's kitchen table and he placed a big bowl of friend potatoes, a bowl of salad and a big platter of fried bluegill fillets on the table. We all dug in and in less than fifteen minutes the food was gone.

Harry laughed and shook his head. "I'd forgotten how much teenage boys can eat," he said.

"You're a heck of a cook Harry," Noah said.

Julio and I volunteered to wash up and Harry didn't argue. He and Noah sat and talked with us as we cleaned up the dishes and pans. "So, what do you think about hunting this weekend Harry," I said.

"I've been out in the marsh almost every day and I've been seeing more ducks each day," he said.

"Really Harry?" I said. "Does that mean the big flight is coming?"

"Something is happening. I've been seeing teal, wood ducks and widgeon mostly. They're the first to leave when the weather changes. These are teal that summered in the north and if they're leaving it must be cooling down up there. If we start to see some mallards this weekend it might mean the big flight is coming. Watch the river side of your hunting spot tomorrow. If you see blue bills or ring bills that means it's getting cold in the north. I'm not sure what's going on, I've never seen such a warm autumn, so this is kind of hard to figure out."

"But it does mean we should be seeing more ducks than last

weekend," Noah said.

"Oh yeah, you'll see more ducks...lots more."

We went out and sat on Harry's dock at dusk and watched the river. Harry seemed to be thinking and was pretty quiet.

"Is something wrong Harry? Noah asked.

"What? Oh no, I was just thinking about how I'll miss this river and the marsh when I'm gone."

"What do you mean...when you're gone Harry?"

"Nobody lives forever boys," Harry said. "Old Bea and I are getting on in years, we won't be here forever."

None of us said anything else. It was hard to think of Harry being gone. We'd just found this amazing man and had learned so much from him that the idea of him dying was hard to think about. I felt an emptiness in my stomach just thinking about Harry being gone.

On the way back to my house we were all pretty excited by Harry's news about the ducks coming. The previous weekend had tried our duck hunting patience to the limit. We were really looking forward to a lot more action this weekend.

"I've got an idea," Noah said.

I looked at him and grinned. "I can't wait," I said.

"Why don't we see how the hunting is tomorrow and then if it's good we can pack extra lunch for Sunday and Monday and take our sleeping bags to the blind and sleep out there Sunday night?"

"Holy smokes, that sounds like fun," I said.

"No kidding," Julio said, "we'll be all ready first thing Monday morning and when other hunters are getting to their blinds they'll scare up ducks to us and we'll be waiting for them."

Now we were even more excited about the upcoming weekend. We decided to let it go until Saturday night before we told our parents and Gram about sleeping in the blind, just in case they didn't go for the idea, we wouldn't give them too long to think about it.

"Do you think we should stop at the hardware store and buy a few more shells?" I asked.

"We didn't shoot any last weekend," Noah said.

"Yeah, but if this is the weekend the ducks come I'd hate to run out especially if we stay out Sunday night and hunt straight through to Monday night."

"You've got that right. Anyone got any money?" I asked.

Between us we had enough for two boxes of shells so we stopped and bought them. That gave us 50 extra shots and if Harry was right, it could mean a lot more ducks for us. If not, they'd keep.

We were all pretty excited when we crawled into bed. The dogs must have sensed something was up because they both galloped around the bedroom for a long time before we could get them settled down.

"This'll be a weekend we'll remember for a long time," I said as I turned out the light. Little did I know how true that statement would turn out to be.

CHAPTER 34

SATURDAY DAWNED WARM and bright. We got up at the usual time and had breakfast and hurried down to the boat dock. By the time we were at the blind the sky was beginning to brighten in the east. Julio and I ran up to the blind and got the decoys and then Noah and I set them out while Julio got the blind ready. We put the puddle ducks in the pond and then set out the string of blue bills and a little group of canvasbacks. I looked over our spread and it looked pretty enticing.

Just as we turned into the cut by our blind a dozen or so teal came zooming over our heads. "Dang, those little guys are up early," I said to Noah.

He nodded and goosed the boat a little faster to get us on the island so we could stash the boat and get to the blind. The dogs were sniffing around and we called them and they crossed the bridge and we closed the door. Julio had the guns loaded and the top of the blind opened up.

"Did you see those ducks come right over your heads?" he asked excitedly.

"Yeah, and I'm glad you didn't shoot at them or you might have shot my head off," I said grinning.

We sat on our stools and soon began to hear shooting all over the marsh. In no time we saw ducks in the sky all over the place. "Oh boy, Harry was right," I said.

Soon a small flock of wood ducks came past us. We heard one of the hens peeping like they do and were ready for them. Just as they came over our pond we stood up and began shooting. The flock scattered like leaves in a hurricane and a few seconds later 4 ducks lay on the pond and the rest were off flying down the marsh. "Holy cow, that was great!" Noah said.

I opened up the dog door and the dogs ran down the bridge and jumped into the water. Kate swam up to a drake and picked him up and Karen grabbed a hen by the wing and began towing her back. When Kate got back she dropped the drake on the shore and jumped into the water again and swam to the other hen. She picked up the duck and then swam over to the second drake. She looked it over a bit and then pushed it up next to a muskrat house with her nose and worked it into her mouth along with the hen.

"Look at that! Kate's bringing both of them in," I said.

Here came Kate with a duck hanging out of each side of her mouth. We all laughed as she came trotting across the bridge. She dropped the ducks on the floor of the blind and stood there wagging her tail.

"Good girl," I said scratching her ears. Kate's tail was going full speed.

From then on the action was just about non-stop. We'd see ducks coming and most would zip over our decoys as if they were looking for friends.

"Harry said these new ducks would be easy to decoy but I didn't think they'd be this easy," I said.

"They haven't been shot at much," Noah said. "They'll get more wary as they get shot at more."

By about eleven o'clock the action slowed down a little. The ducks were probably out feeding in the hills and fields. We sat and had a sandwich and some hot chocolate. "Jeez that was fun," Julio said.

"Lots better than last weekend," I said.

"Did you hear Marco shooting? I think he even got some ducks," Julio said.

"He didn't sky bust them so I'm ok with him shooting," Noah said. "Maybe he changed his attitude."

Julio grinned. "Maybe so...I think he's a little scared of you now."

Noah smiled. "Who me?"

About two o'clock the shooting increased and from then until dusk it was pretty much a circus. There were ducks everywhere and hunters were having a great day shooting at them. We had 19 in the blind and decided it was time to stop when the others stopped shooting. "It's getting too dark," I said.

"If we shoot one now we probably won't find it and I hate to see them go to waste," Julio said.

Noah and I went to pick up the decoys and Julio closed up the blind. We carried the decoys up and stored them inside and then locked up.

On the way back I said to the others, "I think we definitely want to sleep over out here tomorrow night."

"What do you think our parents will say?" Noah said.

"I'm not so worried about them. I'm worried about Gram. She seems to think there's some impending doom coming. She keeps talking about the squirrels and birds and that a big weather change is coming."

"When we get back I'll ask my mom to make us some soup and we can take our little kerosene stove and lantern with us. Then we can sneak out the sleeping bags and tell your mom and not say anything to Gram," he replied.

"Oh man she'll be mad when we get home," I said.

"Not if we come back with a big bag full of ducks."

When we got back to the fish market Noah asked his mom to make us some soup and she said she'd put it in a kettle with a tight lid and we could pick it up in the morning on the way hunting. Noah told her we were going to sleep in the blind and she wasn't too happy about it but decided it would be ok as long as we were careful.

"It's like a little house Mom," Noah said. "It's just about as safe as being right here."

I don't think she was convinced but she said it would be ok. Now all we had to do was get past Gram.

CHAPTER 35

GRAM WAS IMPRESSED with all of our ducks. She decided we should take part of them to Julio's family so we left 9 with her and took the rest to Julio's. While we were there he got his sleeping bag and some cookies and fruit from his mom for lunch. While we were in town we decided we'd better get more shells for Sunday and Monday. We'd shot up almost all of the ones we had during the day.

Between us we had enough money for six more boxes so we bought them and were carrying them down the street with all the rest of our gear when a horn sounded behind us. It was Harry.

"You guys need a lift?" he said as he pulled alongside us.

"Yeah we do Harry," I said.

"Jump into the back," he said. "Are you going to your house?"

"Can you take us to the fish market Harry?" Noah asked.

"No problem, hang on," Harry said.

When we pulled into the fish market we jumped out and put the gear and food into the fish house. "We're taking sleeping bags tomorrow and staying on the river overnight," I said to Harry.

The old man grinned. "Sounds like a lot of fun. What are you going to do with all your ducks?"

We looked confused. "I mean the ducks you shoot tomorrow, how are you going to take care of them?"

"Oh crap, we didn't think of that," Noah said.

"You guys know where I hunt. Why don't one of you bring the ducks up to me at quitting time and I'll take them home with me and quick dress them and put them in the cooler."

"That'd be great Harry," Noah said.

"Not a problem. I think tomorrow is going to be a big day on the river. There were a lot of new ducks out there today. The big flight is on."

"We got 19 today Harry," Julio said.

"Wow, that's good."

"How'd you do today Harry?" I asked.

"Oh pretty good I got about what you did or a few more."

We looked at each other. He shot as many as the three of us combined.

Harry grinned. "Experience," he said.

Harry dropped us off at my house and after an evening of reliving the day's hunt we went up to bed. We were all pretty excited about the hunt tomorrow and we lay awake for over an hour talking and making plans.

Finally, Julio fell asleep and then I heard Kate snoring. I looked over at Noah and he turned toward me. "I'm sure glad we invited Julio to hunt with us," he whispered.

I nodded. "Me too, he's a cool guy."

Noah smiled and turned over on his side. "G'night," he said.

Kate's tail was slapping the bed. It was still dark out but I knew it had to be close to time to get up. Then I heard a noise come from Julio's bed.

Noah began to giggle. "Julio did you roll over on a frog?" he asked.

Julio began to laugh. "Oops, sorry did you hear that?"

"Gram probably heard that," I said.

"It was Karen," he said laughing.

We got up and took turns in the bathroom and trooped down the stairs. Gram was up and there was a pile of pancakes on the table. "I'll be glad when this duck season is over," she said. "Then I can get some sleep on weekends."

Noah went over and put his arms around the old lady and hugged her. He kissed her on the cheek. "You know you like to cook for us," he grinned.

Gram took her spatula and slapped him on the hand. "Don't be silly you goofy Dane," she scolded.

Noah laughed and kissed her again and sat down at the table.

We all began to eat and when we were finished we thanked Gram and grabbed our lunch sack and other gear and headed for the door.

"You guys take a heavy jacket with you today," she said.

"Gram it's 50 degrees out. We're fine in these canvas jackets."

"Listen to me. I know you guys think I'm a crazy old lady but I've seen a lot of falls come and go. When the animals tell you something is coming, I've learned to listen to them. The squirrels are working their little butts off storing nuts. The chickadees and blue jays are hauling sunflower seeds off by the mouthful. The caterpillars are crawling all over looking for a place to cocoon up. Bad weather is coming and you'll make an old lady happy if you take an extra jacket along. What harm can it do?"

"You're right, it's not a problem," I said. I ran upstairs and got my heavy jacket and an old one for Julio. "We'll stop and get Noah one at his house...I promise."

Gram smiled. "Good, now go shoot some ducks."

We got to the fish market and Noah went in the house and got a jacket while Julio and I loaded the kerosene stove, lantern, soup and our shells and other gear. The boat was way too full to be safe and we were standing there looking at it when Steffen came out of the house.

"You guys look a little overloaded," he said.

"We've got more stuff than usual," Noah said. "We're staying in the blind tonight so we accumulated a bit more gear."

"Take the big boat," Steffen said. "I don't need it today. I've only got a couple of nets out and one setline. The ice is going to come soon and I don't want a lot of gear to get frozen under it. I can go out on Tuesday and get my gear."

"Are you sure Dad?"

"Yeah, take the big boat it'll be safer with all that extra weight."

We transferred the gear to the big boat and Noah fired it up. Steffen waved to us as we left the channel to the fish market and started out across the marsh. We were about fifteen minutes later than we'd liked to have been and it was getting light already. We could see ducks flying all over the place and by the time we got to the blind there was shooting from many parts of the marsh.

"Hurry up and get the decoys," Noah said as we unloaded the gear. Julio ran up to the blind and came running with the puddle ducks and then ran back up and got the diving ducks. I had the rest of the stuff on the bank, jumped into the boat and we took off leaving Julio to haul the stuff to the blind.

Noah and I made good time setting out the decoys and by the time we'd finished Julio had everything ready. We pulled the boat up on the bank and were walking up to the bridge when Julio jumped up and shot a pair of mallards out of the sky as they came over our decoys. "Oh guys, would you send the dogs out for my ducks?" he said with a huge grin as his head popped up over the top of the blind.

"Jeez, talk about being greedy," I said. "We do all the work and you shoot all the ducks."

"Get down!" Julio said.

We ducked down and he jumped up and shot another mallard that had strayed too close. We could hear him laughing as we crossed the bridge.

CHAPTER 36

TO SAY THE HUNTING Saturday was good would have been the understatement of the year. The hunting was fabulous. Right after Noah and I got into the blind we began having ducks pass over our decoys. There were teal, widgeon, mallards, wood ducks and once a flock of ducks that looked like they were all hen mallards came past. After a while talking about it we decided they were gadwalls. About noon a big flock of pintails came down the channel and swung past our blind. I shot a drake and a hen and Noah got another drake. When the dogs brought them in we were impressed with their beauty.

"Wow those are even more impressive than those big drake mallards," I said admiring the long tail feathers and the white markings on the big duck.

"I wish we had those around here all year long," Julio said.

"You know what this means," I said. "The flight is on."

By noon the action slowed a little but we still had ducks flying past and heard shooting all over the marsh. There must have been a hundred duck hunters in that ten miles of river and every one of them was having the best day of the season like we were doing.

About mid-afternoon a flight of medium sized ducks came down the river pretty low and buzzed our diving duck decoys. We were kind of caught off guard and they went past without us firing a shot. It wasn't long and another flock came down the river and swung over the decoys and we were ready. We stood up and dropped three of them from the flock. They were in the current and began floating downriver pretty fast so we kept Kate from going after them.

"I'll take Kate and Karen in the boat and go after them," Noah said and he and the dogs did just that. He was downriver a hundred yards when another flock came past and Julio and I dropped two more.

"Hey Noah, why don't you just park down there and we'll shoot them and let them drift down to you," I shouted.

Noah held up his middle finger.

When he got back to the blind we looked at the new ducks and decided they were blue bills. They had a slate blue beak and feet. "Pretty cool little ducks," I said looking one over. "Look how little their wings are compared to a puddle duck like a wood duck," I said.

These were the first diving ducks we'd ever shot so we were pretty excited about seeing more of them and maybe more divers like canvasbacks and golden eyes.

The day wore on and we shot ducks, missed ducks and had a wonderful time. We finally had to take turns eating our lunch because the action never really came to a halt. By dusk we had almost 30 ducks in the blind.

"I better take these to Harry," Noah said.

"I hate to see him have to take care of all those," I said.

"Me too but we can't leave them all night with it being so warm," he replied.

"I'll go with you and we can help him dress them and then come back here."

Julio stayed behind with the dogs and Noah and I went upriver to Harry's little island. Harry was sitting on the edge of his boat scratching Bea's ears.

There was a pile of ducks at least as big as ours in the bottom of his boat. "Holy smokes Harry, you did ok again didn't you?"

"It was a pretty good day. Looks like you guys did ok too."

"We got some blue bills too," I said.

"I saw some of them flying the channel but they don't usually come back into the marsh this far. Well toss those ducks into my boat and I'll head home."

"We'll come with you Harry and help you," Noah said.

"Oh no I'll have those fixed up in a short time. All I'm going to do is pull their guts out and pack them in the cooler. That way they can be picked later. It won't take long at all."

"Are you sure? We hate to have you do all that work."

"Don't worry I've done it a thousand times."

So we transferred our ducks to Harry's boat and he bid us a good night. "Tomorrow will be a day we'll all remember for a long time," he said as he disappeared into the darkness.

Harry had put his little motor on his duck boat and we watched him as he headed upriver. It was almost pitch dark and the old man and his old dog were as at home as if they were in their own living room. I smiled as I watched them disappear.

"Quite a guy isn't he?" I said quietly.

We headed back to our blind and it looked pretty inviting with the light from the lantern showing through the open roof. Julio heard us coming and waved.

"Supper's ready, come and get it."

We parked the boat and were walking up the shore when Noah said, "I wonder if Harry is right, tomorrow is the day?"

"Harry should know," I said. "He's been hunting these bottoms for 60 years."

"Do you ever think it might be a good idea for him to have a hunting companion?" Noah said.

"I've thought about it but you know Harry, he'd never admit he was getting old and couldn't do something on his own."

Noah nodded. "It just makes me think that we should keep an eye on him, just in case."

We got into the blind and Julio had the soup heated up and everything ready for supper. We'd decided to save time in the morning by leaving the decoys out on the water. It made for more room in the blind too. After we ate and fed the dogs we sat and talked and laughed for hours. It began to get chilly so we shut the top of the blind. After a while we all took a trip to the woods, let the dogs to potty and then shut up the blind. We spread our sleeping bags on the floor and lay down.

"This is the coolest thing I've ever done I think," Julio said.

"I'm glad you've been hunting with us," I said.

"Me too," Noah said.

"Thanks guys. I'm glad you gave me a chance after how Marco acted. You know sometimes he can be real nice but for some reason he has a chip on his shoulder. I hope he gets over whatever he's angry about. I think you guys would really like him if you got to know him."

"We'll see," Noah said grinning.

"I'm not holding my breath," I said.

We shut off the lantern and lay there listening to the sound of the river flowing under the tree the blind was built on. "Wow," I thought to myself, "what an adventure this has been. This will be something we'll tell our kids about years from now."

I had no idea how true that statement would turn out to be.

CHAPTER 37

Armistice Day

I WOKE AND IT WAS STILL DARK, but I knew it was getting close to the time to get up because I had to pee real badly. There was enough light in the blind to see the dogs curled up together and Noah and Julio on either side of me sleeping. I tried to ignore my need to get up and finally couldn't wait any longer. I slipped from my sleeping bag and opened the door of the blind and tiptoed out across the bridge barefoot and in my underwear. It was a warm breezy morning and the sky was just beginning to brighten in the east.

I did my business and went back to the blind. When I opened the door Noah and Julio were lying in their sleeping bags talking.

"So what does it look like out there?" Julio asked.

"Beautiful morning," I said, "not a cloud in the sky from what I can see."

"We better get up and have a little snack and get ready," Noah said. "If Harry was right, we'll be busy today shooting ducks."

We rolled up the sleeping bags and stowed them in the corner of the blind. Noah and Julio took the dogs out and all of them went potty. When they came back I had the stove going and had poured a thermos of hot chocolate into the pan so we could heat it back up. We had some sandwiches and fruit and then got dressed and opened the roof of the blind.

It was still pretty dark but you could begin to make out features in the landscape. We could see muskrat houses, the edge of the pond and the decoys sitting silent on the water. I picked up a box of shells and began shoving some into my gun when there was a shot from upriver in the marsh, pretty close to us.

Suddenly the marsh was full of quacking and the sound of wings splashing on water. We stood there transfixed as the air slowly became filled with ducks. They were rising up out of little puddles and ponds all over the area, scared up by the sound of the gun being discharged.

"Holy smokes!" Noah said, grabbing for his gun.

"My gosh where did all of those come from?" Julio said looking from one side to the other.

"They must have come in after dark," Noah said shaking his head from side to side unbelievingly.

There had to be 300 ducks in the air. We scrambled around and soon there was shooting all over the marsh and more ducks rose up from the grass. Ducks came past us and we began to shoot. The dogs were scrambling out of the blind to fetch those that we'd shot. Kate brought a mallard back and went right out again. Karen was dragging her first duck in toward the blind.

For the next half hour it was chaos. We shot, loaded our guns, shot some more and re-loaded. There were ducks everywhere. Eventually the shooting in the marsh slowed down as the ducks left for the fields and streams in the hills. There were still many flying around but the big early morning run was over. Kate was carrying a mallard in and Karen was carrying a teal. We stopped for a breather and just looked stunned at each other.

"I didn't think there were that many ducks on the whole river, let alone right here," Noah said.

"How many did we get?" I asked.

We began to check the pile of ducks on the floor of the blind and found we had 11 piled up with the dogs coming in with another two.

"I'll take the boat and check the weeds with Kate," Noah said.

He and Kate went out looking for more ducks that hadn't fallen in the water. Noah went along the edge of the weeds and Kate stood in front of the boat sniffing the air. I could hear her nose working and she sounded like a pig grunting. Suddenly she leaped over the side of the boat and into the grass and a few seconds later she reappeared with a duck in her mouth. Noah reached over the side of the boat and took the duck from Kate.

She turned around and went back into the grass. We watched as Kate rummaged around in the weeds and in fifteen minutes they came back with another 6 birds.

"Jeez, that's amazing," I said. "Harry was right, today is the day."

By now the sun was up and there was a gentle breeze blowing upriver from the south. We were in our shirtsleeves since it was warm and comfortable.

"It's gotta be at least 60 degrees," Julio said wiping a sheen of sweat from his forehead.

Ducks began to come back to the marsh from their feeding areas and we began to shoot again. All over the river we could hear hunters shooting at ducks. It sounded like every duck hunter in the state was out hunting.

It wasn't long and we began to see huge flocks of ducks flying down the river from the north. These weren't just little family groups of a dozen ducks but huge flocks that might have held over a hundred birds. We were amazed by the numbers of them that kept increasing by the minute. We could look almost any direction and see between five hundred and a thousand ducks at any one time.

"I didn't know there were this many ducks in the whole world," I said.

"They're all coming at once," Noah said. "This will be a day we'll never forget."

By about 11 o'clock the sun began to disappear in high fluffy clouds and the wind began to switch around and come from the northwest. The numbers of ducks grew even larger as flock after flock funneled down the river. The flocks were now constantly appearing and flying past us. At any one minute we could probably see several thousand ducks in the air.

We shot, reloaded, shot, reloaded and shot some more. The sound of guns firing was constant, like something I'd expect to hear if a war was going on. The dogs were running themselves ragged trying to keep up with us.

We saw every kind of duck that lived in North America. The huge majority of the ducks were mallards but now we were seeing more ducks flying out over the channel. There were thousands of blue bills in flocks as big as a couple of hundred. Then we saw huge flocks of big gray ducks with a reddish head.

"Those have to be canvasbacks," Noah said.

Soon we saw golden eyes, buffleheads, and what we thought were redheads. Most of the diving ducks were out away from us too far but every now and then there was a flock that came over and we shot at them.

I began to worry about running out of shells.

"How many bullets do we have left?" I asked Noah.

He took a quick count. "Looks like almost three boxes, it's a good thing we stopped the other day and got extras."

The sky now was getting dark and forbidding looking and the wind had picked up considerably. The river was beginning to show whitecaps and the air was cooling off. Still no one paid attention to the deteriorating conditions. The shooting kept up and the ducks kept coming.

"Look at that!" Noah said pointing to the west.

I looked and saw a huge flock of geese. Behind them were more and more flocks of the huge birds.

"I hope a few of them come past," I said.

In the next half hour we probably saw ten thousand geese fly past us. The wind picked up and it began to rain a little. The whitecaps on the river were building up and some were three feet or more. We put our canvas jackets on over our flannel shirts. A flock of geese came past just at the minimum altitude for us to get a shot but we all missed.

Then I heard another new sound from the air and looked up to see about 200 white swans flying overhead.

"Holy smokes look at that!"

"Harry said those are the last to migrate," Julio said.

"I guess it's pretty nasty up north," I replied.

Little did I know just how nasty.

CHAPTER 38

THE SOUND OF SHOTGUNS firing was almost constant. It seemed that every duck hunter in the area was on the river and every duck and goose in North America was flying down the river. The wind increased and suddenly I felt a sharp stinging on my face and realized that the rain had turned to sleet. Noah looked at me with an uncomfortable look on his face.

"It's getting pretty nasty," he said, "I wonder if we should let the dogs go out any more. The waves are getting pretty big."

I looked down at the water and sure enough, the waves coming down the channel of the main river were now four foot whitecaps and were growing in size by the minute. Kate looked bushed but wasn't about to let any ducks get away if she could help it.

"We better not shoot at any on the river side from now on it's getting too rough out there. I'm afraid Kate would get in that choppy water and drown."

"Let's close the dog door," Noah said. "If we get some ducks down we'll take the boat after them, I don't want Kate to get caught in the wind and current. Kate's a good swimmer but I'm afraid Karen couldn't keep up."

I nodded and closed the dog door. The two dogs looked up at us with strange expressions on their faces but I think they were actually relieved that they didn't have to go out again. They were dead tired.

"Lay down Kate," I said. "Take a rest old girl."

We were down to less than one box of shells. We decided that we'd only shoot at ducks on the inside of the island in the pond and ones that we knew would land close to us if we got them. It was just too rough out in the river channel where the waves were now up to three or four feet high.

The sleet suddenly turned into snow. At first it was just a fairly thin snowfall with tiny delicate flakes but within a few minutes it was almost a whiteout.

The sky turned almost solid white as the snow turned heavy and so thick that we could barely see the decoys on the water.

"This is getting bad," I said.

Noah nodded. Julio said, "Do you think we should leave?"

I looked at Noah. "I think for the time being, we're safer here in this blind than we'd be out in the boat," I said.

Noah agreed. "Let's wait until we're out of shells and see what it's like. Then we can decide.

"Besides this'll probably blow over soon and if we left we'd feel stupid for going when the shooting was so good," I said.

The shooting was still going strong out across the marsh and the ducks were everywhere. Any direction you looked you would see hundreds of ducks flying one way or the other as the snow would let up for a second. They were all looking for a place to take shelter and every time they tried to land in a sheltered pond, someone would shoot at them and they'd go up in the air again. We each had two shells left in our guns. The rest of the empty hulls were scattered over the floor of the blind.

A flock of mallards circled our decoys and set their wings and we stood and shot at them. We knocked two drakes from the flock and that was it for our shooting...our shells were gone.

"I'll go fire up the boat," Noah said.

He opened the door and carefully walked across the snow covered bridge. "You want to go with him or want me to?" I said to Julio.

"I'll go, why don't you start to get stuff together so we can get out of here?"

Julio buttoned up the collar of his canvas coat and went out the door. I began putting things in order in the blind and then looked over the side to see what they were doing. Noah was piloting the boat through the decoys and Julio was in front directing him. The snow was coming down so hard they couldn't see where they were going. Finally I saw Julio pick a duck out of the water and they turned around and headed back to the island. A few minutes later they came into the blind.

"Man it's like a hurricane out there," Noah said brushing show off his shoulders. I think we should close up the blind and think about getting home."

Julio and I agreed and we struggled to get the roof folded down against the wind. When we finally had it secured we opened the door and let the dogs out. They tiptoed across the bridge and headed for the boat. We were right behind them.

Noah was already in the boat when we heard the outboard. I stopped and turned my head to listen. We could only see a few feet out across the water and weren't sure where the sound was coming from.

"Do you hear that?" I said to Julio.

He nodded and pointed toward the river channel. "It sounds like somebody is coming down the channel. Holy cow they're crazy if they think they can make it in those waves."

We turned toward the river side of the island and saw huge waves pounding down the channel. Some looked to be six or seven feet tall. They were breaking on the outside of the island and throwing up huge geysers of spray into the trees where it froze almost on contact. Thankfully we'd built our blind up high enough that only the bottom of the boards were getting wet by the waves and the rest of the blind was pretty safe looking...yet.

Then we heard the whine of the motor again and I saw a small boat with a lone hunter in it, coming toward the cut in the island. "He's going to try to get through the cut," I said to Julio.

"He better time it right or one of those big waves will swamp him," Julio said shaking his head.

We could barely see the guy through the snow and knew he was in big trouble. The waves were crashing into the cut and he'd have to take them from the side as he turned into the pond. If one of them hit him in the side, he'd be in big trouble.

Suddenly Julio grabbed my sleeve and looked very frightened. "Oh my gosh it's Marco!" he said.

CHAPTER 39

NOAH HAD THE MOTOR RUNNING and was below us so he had no idea of what was happening on the other side of the island. Kate had jumped into the boat and Karen was standing up with her paws on the gunwale waiting for a lift.

"Are you guys coming?" he yelled over the howl of the wind.

I think I was holding my breath when Marco started to turn the boat. He was in really bad trouble and the slightest mistake was going to end up with him in the river. The wind was howling and the snow was blowing so hard that we lost sight of Marco for a half a minute but when we saw him again he was turning to try to come into the back side of the island.

"Oh man," Julio said more to himself than to me.

Marco timed it right on the first wave and rode over the crest. Once it was past him he turned across the waves and tried to make for safety. The wind was blowing hard enough that the boat didn't respond as quickly as needed and the second wave hit Marco dead on and crashed over the boat, filling it with icy water. We could see him desperately trying to get turned but it wasn't going to happen. Another wave followed the last and when it hit him the boat turned over like a turtle.

"Marco!" Julio yelled. He took off running toward the end of the island. We could see the bottom of the boat as it washed downriver in the waves but couldn't see Marco anywhere.

I ran down the island to the boat. "Noah, we gotta go!" I yelled and pushed the boat off the island while jumping in. Karen fell into the water and looked at me wondering why I didn't lift her I suppose but I had much bigger worries right then. "Marco just capsized his boat outside of our cut, he's in the water!"

Noah put the boat in reverse and backed us up quickly from the island and then put it into gear and we roared around the tree with our blind and out into the main channel. As soon as we rounded the tree the waves began to slam into us. They were at least six feet high and stacked up one after the other slamming into the shore every few seconds.

"Which way?" Noah shouted.

I could just make out Julio through the snow. "Can you see him?" I yelled.

"I saw him hanging onto the boat a minute ago but they drifted downriver, I can't see him anymore!"

I motioned for Noah to go downriver. We turned and got going with the waves and it wasn't as bad. A couple of seconds later I saw the shaft of Marco's motor sticking up a little way from the water. The boat was upside down but the shaft was still visible. I pointed frantically and Noah went the way I was pointing. Just then I saw Marco come to the surface. He was trying to swim but not making any head ways against the waves and current. He turned and saw us but suddenly he disappeared under the water.

"Noah, over there!" I yelled pointing at the spot Marco had disappeared. Noah gave the engine gas and we shot forward. Marco came up again and then went down. Kate was standing with her feet on the front edge of the boat and she went over the side a second later.

"Kate! Kate, come back here!" I yelled but it was no use. She was on a mission and no one was going to stop her. "Follow Kate," I yelled to Noah.

We caught up to Kate and she had Marco's wrist in her mouth trying to make for the island. I reached over the side of the boat and grabbed his hand and Noah ran forward and grabbed Kate by the back of the neck. He got her lifted part way up and then grabbed her around the chest and heaved her into the boat. I was trying lift Marco but he was too heavy for me. Noah got along side me and grabbed farther up his sleeve and with a few good heaves we managed to haul him aboard. He looked like he was dead. His face was as white as the snow and his eyes were closed.

Noah ran back to the motor and gave it gas. "Hang on I'm going to turn into the waves," he said.

I knelt by Marco and shook him. "Marco, come on, Marco!" I leaned down to see if I could hear his heartbeat but the wind and the motor noise was too loud. I pulled open his jacket and ripped his shirt open and put my hand on his bare chest and I could feel his heart beating. "He's alive!" I yelled to Noah.

I stayed kneeling in the bottom of the boat because we were taking a beating from the waves and wind. The big boat would slam into each wave, ride it up and then smash through on the back side of it. It seemed like we were going to go right up in the air and over on our backs each time and it was only because Noah knew just when to give it gas and when to back off that we didn't capsize.

Slowly but surely we made it back to the cut where the blind was and turned into the relatively calm water behind the island. Julio was standing there with Karen in his arms with tears running down his face. "Is he dead?" he asked.

I shook my head no. "He's unconscious but he's alive. We've got to get him warmed up really quickly. Go fire up the lantern and the kerosene stove and find all the dry stuff we have."

Julio ran for the blind, worked his way across the snow covered bridge and opened the door. Noah shut down the motor and came forward. "You think he'll be ok?"

"I think so if we can get him warmed up. He's probably got hypothermia. We have to take him into the blind and see what we can do. If we set out for home with him wet like this he'll die for sure."

Noah nodded in agreement. He got out onto the shore and I lifted Marco's legs up to the edge of the boat. Noah grabbed his feet and I stood up and we lifted him to the front deck. I got out of the boat and we lifted again and moved him to the shore. "Jeez, he weighs a ton," Noah said gasping as we lifted.

We half lifted, half dragged Marco through the snow to the bridge. Julio came out the door just as we got there and he helped me take the front half of his brother and we carefully carried him across the bridge.

"Jeez, don't drop him in that hole down there," Julio said. "He'd be a goner for sure."

We burst out laughing. It wasn't really funny but we needed it after the intense last few minutes. When we got inside we lay Marco on the floor of the blind. I went back and yelled at Kate who was standing on the end of the bridge.

"Come on girl, you can make it."

Kate carefully tiptoed across the snowy bridge and then came into the blind wagging her tail enthusiastically. "You did good old girl," I said hugging the wet dog.

Noah shook his head. "What a brave girl," he said. "You saved his life Kate."

I ran back across the bridge and picked up Karen and carried her into the blind.

"We gotta get Marco dried out." I said.

"You guys are all wet too," Julio said looking at our clothes.

"We're not soaked through like him. I'm still dry underneath, how about you Noah?"

"Yeah, my jacket and shirt are wet but I've got a T shirt and my jeans are ok. I think we should strip his wet clothes off and get him into a sleeping bag. Then if we close up the door and let the stove work we can heat him up. I'm gonna run down and get the boat tied up so it doesn't get blown off the island," Noah said.

I closed the door and latched it when Noah had gone. Julio looked up at me. "I'll undress him he's my brother I guess."

I grinned at him. "Don't worry Julio I'm sure he won't mind."

Noah came back and knocked on the door and I let him in. "It's getting really bad. The wind is like a hurricane."

Noah helped Julio get Marco's clothes and shoes off and I took an old cloth lunch bag that we'd left behind and dried Kate off as well as I could. She shook and seemed pretty comfortable.

She and Karen lay down by the stove and in a few minutes they were both sleeping. Julio and Noah had Marco naked and they took another lunch bag and dried him off. I unzipped a sleeping bag all the way open and we lifted Marco onto one half and then zipped up the bag with him inside.

"You think that'll be warm enough?" Noah asked.

"I think he needs body heat to warm him up." I looked at Julio. "He's your brother," I said.

"But he's naked."

"Julio it's not like you're going to marry him, it's just to warm him up."

Julio sighed and sat down and took off his boots. "I don't have to strip down do I?"

Noah and I laughed. "Just take off your jacket and shoes. Then get as close to him as you can and let him thaw out."

Julio did as we said and slid down into the sleeping bag with Marco. "Jeez, it's like being in here with a big ice cube."

Noah and I grinned. "Be gentle," I said. Julio wasn't amused.

CHAPTER 40

THE BLIND WASN'T WHAT YOU'D CALL HOT but it was much warmer than being in the wind and snow outside. Noah and I took off our shirts and canvas jackets and put on two of the heavy coats Gram had made us bring along. Then I grabbed an old hammer and a coffee can of nails we'd left in the blind in case of emergency repairs and drove several nails into the front wall of the blind near the heater. We hung our jackets and shirts on some of the nails and then looked down at Marco's soaked clothes.

"We should take them outside and wring them out as well as we can and maybe they'll dry eventually," Noah said.

I nodded. "Julio stay put, we're going to take these out and we'll be right back."

We gathered up the clothes and Noah opened the door. The wind whipped in and snow billowed in through the opening. Noah moved out onto the bridge and I followed. We took each item of Marco's clothes and twisted them opposite ways until most of the water ran out onto the bridge. The water froze almost instantly.

"It's getting colder and colder," I said.

"There's no way we can make it home tonight," Noah said looking off into the darkness. "In this snow we'd never be able to find our way."

"We've got to stay here," I agreed. "At least we'll be warm and dry. I hate to think of being out in this and not have some shelter."

Noah shook his head. "It'd be impossible to survive," he said.

The wind was blowing at least 60 or 70 miles per hour. Had we not been behind the blind we couldn't have stood up on the bridge without being blown off into the river. The snow was coming down so hard you couldn't see the island past the end of the bridge. It was like being in the Arctic. Just then I thought I heard something and I turned my head.

"Noah did you hear that?"

Noah turned and put his hand up to his ear to cup the sound. He nodded. "Way down river, it sounds like someone yelling for help."

"Oh God, oh my God," I whispered. I felt sick to my stomach. Just thinking of someone out there in the darkness with the snow and wind made me almost sick.

We went inside and hung Marco's clothes up on more nails. Julio had dropped off to sleep and opened his eyes when we came in. "Is it still snowing?"

"Harder than ever," Noah said. "The wind is like wind I've never seen. Man, its bad out there."

"We aren't going to try to make it back are we?"

"No way," I said. "We're dry and fairly warm here. We'll wait it out. It can't snow forever."

Julio and I were talking and I noticed Marco moving around in the sleeping bag. Suddenly his eyes opened and he looked confused and frightened. He looked at his brother next to him in the sleeping bag. "Julio what the hell are you doing?"

"I'm thawing you out you big dummy," Julio said.

"What the...? Where am I?"

"You're in our duck blind."

I could see on Marco's face that he noticed he was naked. "What the heck happened? Where are my clothes? How did I get in here?"

"You were trying to get here in your boat I guess, we saw you coming down the river and you capsized right out in the channel by our blind. Noah and Sebastian went out to try to help you. Sebastian's dog jumped in and grabbed your arm as you went under and she held you up until they could drag you into the boat. Then we got you in here, took off your wet clothes and I got in here to warm you up. I don't like it any better than you do," Julio said.

162

Marco was trying to digest all of this information. He looked up at Noah and me. "You guys came after me? After all the stuff I did to you, you still came to help me?"

"You were in trouble Marco," I said. "It didn't matter who you were, we had to try to help you."

Marco looked at Noah. "Pederson, I'm sorry about all the stupid shit I did, man I feel like a real dope. Thanks guys, thanks so much."

And then he started to cry.

We all felt kind of embarrassed and tried to make ourselves busy. Marco got himself together and Julio climbed out of the sleeping bag. I grabbed one of the heavy jackets we had left and gave it to Marco. "Here put this on. We don't have any pants for you yet but you can wrap up in the sleeping bag for now."

Marco put the jacket on and then got up and held the sleeping bag around his lower half and sat on one of the stools. "I can't believe I'm here. I knew I wasn't going to be able to make it back to shore. The waves were so big. I've never seen such big waves. I thought maybe you guys would have gone already and left the blind open. I can't believe how lucky I am."

"You're just lucky we were outside when you came past or we'd have never heard you or saw you," Noah said.

"And that old dog came in for me?"

I nodded. "That old dog is one brave old girl. She bailed out of the boat like a lifeguard." I turned to Kate and said, "You're a pretty brave girl aren't you Kate?"

She heard her name and raised her head. She looked at each of us and then lay back down to sleep.

"I guess it's all in a day's work for her," Julio said smiling.

"How much food do we have left?" Noah asked.

Julio and I began rummaging around in the food sacks and came up with some apples and oranges and three sandwiches. There was one thermos of semi-hot chocolate left also. We shared the food with the dogs and all had a pretty good meal.

"So we're going to wait for morning?" I said.

163

Everyone nodded.

Marco said. "I'm not trying to run things but if we let those two heaters run in here we should vent a little of the fumes outside. Kerosene can kill you if you breathe too much of it I think."

"Good idea," I said. "Without them it'll get pretty cold in here. We can wedge something up in the corner of the roof and let a little air in and fumes out. Noah loosened the latch on the roof and we slid a couple of empty shotgun shells into the opening. It wasn't very big but it let in enough fresh air to keep us from getting fumed out.

"I've got to pee before we settle in," Julio said.

"We all should take turns and then we might as well settle in for the night," Noah said.

Marco went out on the bridge first and when he came in he had a strange look on his face. "Way down river I can see a light. It looks like a bonfire. Do you suppose someone got trapped on an island somewhere?"

I went out and sure enough. Way downriver, at least a mile or maybe two, there was a fire going. "Oh man, those guys are in big trouble," I thought to myself.

We all finished going outside and latched the door shut. The wind was still howling and every so often a gust would slam against the blind and shake it. It was kind of unnerving but the blind was solid and we weren't too worried.

We decided that two of us should get into two of the sleeping bags together and then we'd pile the heavy coats and the other sleeping bag on top of us. We made a place between them for the dogs to settle in and we all took off our shoes and coats and got inside. Noah and I were in one bag and the Gianolli boys were in the other. I spread the zipped open bag over the whole nest and we settled in. Kate and Karen were snug between the bags sleeping on a heavy coat with the extra bag over them and us. It was nice and warm and I felt pretty safe.

We were quiet for a while and then Noah said, "I wonder how

many guys are out there stranded?"

"God, I don't know. I hope none but you know that's not true. I wonder if they can live through the night?"

"Marco, do you know Harry Gillette?" I asked.

"The old guy, sure everyone knows Harry."

"You know north of where you were hunting there's a little tree all alone out in the marsh?"

"Yeah some guy was there hunting every time I was out in the marsh. Dang good shot too. He knocked a lot of ducks from the air over there. Why?"

"That was Harry. He hunts there. He's hunted there for years."

"When you realized you were in trouble.....was he still there?"

Marco looked at me. He nodded. "He was still shooting."

My heart felt cold. Harry surely was experienced enough to get out while the getting was still good...wasn't he?

Noah looked at me. "You don't think Harry stayed too long...do you?"

"God, I hope not Noah. I really hope not."

CHAPTER 41

NOAH SLEPT LIKE A LOG but I had a hard time getting to sleep. Across from us Marco was soundly sleeping but Julio was also tossing and turning. The blind rocked and creaked when a blast of wind slammed into it but I wasn't too worried. We'd built it to withstand flood water so we thought it was sturdy enough to stand up against the gale force winds. Occasionally we'd feel a wave slam into the trunk of the tree but nothing had leaked into the blind.

"What time do you think it is?" Julio whispered.

"It's got to be close to morning. It seems like this night took forever," I said.

He nodded. "I'm glad Marco got some sleep. He was pretty well done for when we brought him in here. Man, he's a lucky guy."

"We just happened to be there at the right time," I said. "I wonder how many other guys like him are out there in the dark and cold?"

Julio just shook his head. "I'm afraid what we'll find when tomorrow comes," he said sadly.

I dozed off for a while and then the next time I opened my eyes I could see a little light coming in through the corner of the roof where we'd opened it to let out the fumes. The stove was still burning but the lantern had gone out. Noah moved in his sleep and farted. I began to laugh.

"Jeez, you pig!" I said.

Noah opened his eyes and grinned. "A morning kiss for you," he said grinning. "Is it morning yet?"

I nodded. I think so it sounds like the wind has died down a bit too."

Our talking woke Julio and Marco who both turned our way. "Who crapped themselves?" Julio asked grinning.

I just shook my head. "Guess."

One by one we crawled out of our warm sleeping bags and stretched. The blind wasn't exactly hot but it was warm enough to make us feel comfortable and we felt pretty lucky to be in it. There were a lot of guys out in the marsh who must have spent a hellish night compared to what we had. Marco's boots were still pretty wet but his clothes had dried out so we all dressed. We still had a couple of pairs of hip boots in the corner so he put on a pair of them instead of his regular hunting boots.

"I suppose we should look out and see what its like," I said.

Noah unlatched the door and he and Julio had to push pretty hard against it to move it from all the snow that had drifted behind the blind onto the bridge. They managed to get it open and then Noah took the lid from the kettle we'd had our soup in and used it as a shovel to push the rest of the snow off the bridge.

We all crossed to the island and stood there in knee deep snow.

"Holy cow, everything is frozen up," Marco said surveying the landscape.

We looked toward the river and it was still flowing but there were hundreds of ice chunks floating down it. The pond in back of the island was completely frozen over. There wasn't much snow on the ice because the wind kept it free but behind any obstruction there were snow drifts. Noah looked toward the boat.

"The boat's buried," he said.

"We'll have to dig it out," Julio said.

The wind was now just a strong breeze and the sun was beginning to come up over the bluffs. We waded through the snow to the boat and found it when Marco ran into it and fell down. It was completely buried in a snowdrift that was seven or eight feet deep.

'Wow, this is gonna take some work," I said.

"I wonder if the ice is hard enough to walk on. Maybe we

could walk home easier," Julio said.

"I can't leave Dad's boat out here," Noah said. "It might take some work but we've got to try to dig it out."

Julio went back to the blind and got the pot from the soup and we began digging and throwing snow from the boat. None of us had gloves so we had to stop every few minutes and warm up our hands. We finally cut a couple of the lunch sacks into strips and wrapped them around our hands and it worked a lot better for removing snow. It took us a long time, maybe 3 hours but we finally freed the boat from all the snow.

We were all sweating and panting from the work. "See if it'll start," I said to Noah.

He crawled in and walked to the back and pressed the starter. The engine whined and coughed and died. Noah waited a minute, moved the throttle up and down and then tried it again. This time it whined faster and after one more try it started. We all cheered and slapped each other on the back.

"Let's get the dogs and the guns and try to get home," I said.

Noah stayed with the boat and began to rock it backward and forward trying to break up the ice around it. Marco, Julio and I went up to the blind and put the guns in their cases, pulled down the corner of the blind where we'd opened it for fresh air, turned off the stove and rolled up the sleeping bags.

"We can come back later or maybe next spring to get the rest of this," I said.

We locked up and headed back to the boat. Julio carried Karen because she was so short she couldn't get through the snow. Marco went ahead of Kate and helped her through the deepest drifts. We got the dogs into the boat and Julio and I pushed it away from the island as far as it would go in the water Noah had opened up.

He jockeyed the boat back and forth and got us turned toward the direction we wanted to go. He'd run the boat forward until the ice quit giving away and the boat ran up onto it. Then the three of us would walk forward to the bow and the added weight would make the bow break through. Then we'd go forward again until we ran up on the ice again and repeat the whole thing. It was a slow way to go but we had no other choice.

We had been going for half an hour and turned from one of the channels to another pond that we could cross. Just as we turned the corner Julio shouted, "Look there's a duck boat."

There was a small duck skiff partly sticking up out of the water, its bow on the snow and its stern under the ice.

"Oh no!"

I turned and looked where Marco was pointing. There was a man's hand sticking up out of the snow.

"He must have tipped his boat over and only made it part way up onto land before he froze or passed out," Noah said quietly.

We all sat there looking at the white frozen hand sticking up from the snow. None of us had ever seen a dead person and it was pretty sobering for us.

"There's nothing we can do," I said. "Remember where he is, we'll have to tell someone."

"Who do you think it was?" Marco asked.

"I don't know it's hard to tell by a hand."

"Did you recognize the boat?"

I shook my head. "No, but one thing I do know is that it's not Harry's boat."

But I had a sense of foreboding that made me feel very afraid.

CHAPTER 42

THE SIGHT OF A DEAD MAN shook us up badly. We all had thought about the possibility of someone dying in the storm but it wasn't real until we saw a frozen body. We continued our slow progress across ponds, and up and down channels toward the channel that would lead us to the fish market.

A short while later we heard the sound of a plane flying somewhere near and stopped. "There!" Marco said pointing out over the main channel of the river.

A small plane was flying low over the islands and every now and then he'd drop something from the plane.

"He must be looking for hunters who got stranded," Noah said.

"I wonder what he's dropping?"

Noah shrugged. "Maybe food? Who knows?"

We watched for a long time and saw the pilot drop many packages from the plane. There were a lot more hunters out there than we'd suspected. Finally we continued our slow journey toward the shore. When we came to a channel the ice was very thin and we were able to just break through by motoring slowly. Then when we had to cross another slough or pond we had thicker ice and it was much slower going.

We turned from a channel into a pond that was pretty close to shore. "Look there's somebody!" Julio said.

"Hey mister, wait we can take you in the boat!"

The man was in the water wearing hip boots and was up to about his thighs. He was holding onto a branch from an overhanging tree and facing away from us toward the land. It looked like he was stopped to catch his breath. Noah sped up as much as he could and we got closer.

"Hey mister, hey!"

The man didn't answer nor did he turn our way. I got a bad feeling in my stomach and looked at Marco and Julio who were thinking the same thing I was thinking. We came along side the man and he was frozen solid. He'd grabbed the branch to steady himself and somehow he'd just stopped there and died still hanging onto the branch. We stopped and sat looking at him.

"My God, would you look at that?" Noah said quietly.

I shook my head. "What a terrible way to die. He was alone in the dark and the snow and wind." My eyes filled with tears thinking of the poor man and his horrible death.

"What should we do?" Marco asked.

"We better just leave him and tell the authorities. We already have to tell them about the other guy in the water. Noah, get us out of here," I said.

Noah put the boat in gear and we slowly moved away from the man. As we got farther away we all looked back and just shook our heads. Never....in my life had I expected to see a dead man, and certainly not two in one day.

It was midday by the time we turned into our channel. As soon as they heard the motor Noah's parents, my mom and Gram and Julio's parents all came running down the parking lot toward the dock. There were tears of joy on their faces.

We pulled up to the dock and they came and grabbed us and began kissing us and hugging us. Gram put her arms around me and hugged me and then grabbed my ear and twisted it. "Sleep out there and not tell me?"

I was surprised and shocked and my ear was hurting but I had to laugh. "It was Noah's idea," I said.

Gram let loose of me and went for Noah. He ran through the deep snow and the old lady couldn't keep up to him. It's a wonder he could make it himself since he was laughing so hard.

There was a lot of hugging and talking and we all moved up to the fish market and went inside where it was warm. Julio was telling the story of Kate rescuing Marco and everyone was amazed at the old dog's bravery. Marco's parents both hugged Kate hard and she was happy for the attention but had no idea why everyone was acting that way. After all she saw something to retrieve and did her job. Our families marveled at the luck we'd had getting through the storm.

Gram and Noah's mom began making food and soon we were all in little groups talking and laughing. I suddenly remembered the two hunters who we'd found and asked Steffen if I could use the phone to call the sheriff. I went to the office and called and explained where the two bodies were.

"We're looking for a lot of people right now," he said. "You didn't know either of these men?"

"The one under the ice we couldn't see and the other was a stranger to us."

"We've recovered seven bodies already and there are still many people missing," he said. He thanked me for calling and I hung up. I went back and filled a plate with food. I sat down with Marco and Julio at a table and began eating. Marco was grinning from ear to ear and asked me ten times if he could get me some more of this or that.

"Marco you don't have to wait on me," I said.

"I know but I owe you guys big."

"Let's just let it go at thanks and from now on we'll all be friends instead of enemies," I said.

He shook hands with me and then went and talked to Noah and shook with him. I looked at Noah and he winked at me and grinned.

A while later Steffen came from his office and spoke to my mom quietly. Mom got a worried look on her face and hurried to the office. I watched and wondered what was wrong and a few minutes later she came out and looked like she'd just seen death. She walked over to me and I stood up.

"Sebastian, that was the Sheriff on the phone, he knew we were here because you'd called him."

"What's wrong Mom?"

"Sebastian, your Dad's ship...it sank in the storm."

CHAPTER 43

MY KNEES FELT LIKE RUBBER and I staggered backward when I heard what my mom had said. Noah grabbed me and helped me to a chair.

"What's wrong Bastian?" he said.

I looked up and my eyes began to fill with tears. "Dad's ship," I said.

He looked confused. "What?"

"It went down Noah, it sank."

Noah's mouth dropped open and he turned white. He put his arms around my shoulders and hugged me. "I....I don't know what to say," he stammered.

In the next few minutes our happy reunion had turned very silent and sad. Everyone was whispering and Gram was consoling Mom.

Julio and Marco came over by Noah and me and pulled up chairs so the four of us were all sitting together. They looked miserable and just sat there not saying anything. What could they say?

Finally Mom came over to me. "We better go home in case they hear anything more," she said. "I told the Sheriff we'd be home soon and to call there if there was any new information."

I nodded, got up and turned to my three friends. They all had tears in their eyes and just stepped up and hugged me and I nodded and got my jacket and Mom, Gram and I started walking up the street through the path that had been plowed by the snowplow. Gram had her arm through mine and I helped her through the deep snow.

I hadn't realized how much snow there was until we got a little way up the hill towards my house. In places the drifts had to be fifteen or twenty feet deep. There were humps and mounds in the snow along the road that must have been buried cars. On the downwind side of many of the homes the drifts covered the lower windows on the houses.

Because our house faced into the direction the wind had come from, the front yard was fairly clean of snow. Mom had shoveled a path to the street so we had no trouble getting home. When we got there Gram made some coffee and we sat at the kitchen table waiting for the phone to ring.

"What exactly did the Sheriff say?" I asked.

"He just said the shipping company had called and that the *Novadoc* had broken in half and sunk in the storm. They wanted all families to know."

"Are they sure everyone is gone?"

"They had no more information. All they said was that the ship had been sailing close to the shore trying to stay out of the wind and then it shifted to the southwest and they got caught broadside and ran aground at Little Sable Point lighthouse. The ship broke in half."

"So it ran aground, is it still above water?"

"I don't know Sebastian, that's all they said. They'll let us know more as soon as they know something."

The three of us sat at the kitchen table and the clock ticked loudly. My mind was filled with the thoughts of my dad in the deadly cold water of Lake Michigan and it was almost more than I could take. I heard feet stomping on the porch and looked toward the door. Noah was looking in the window on the door.

I waved to him to come in.

"I just wanted to stop and see if there's anything I can do," he said looking uncomfortable.

"Come on in," I said. "Take off your boots, have some coffee."

Noah looked at Mom and Gram and they both smiled at him. "Come on Noah, you know you're welcome."

He smiled and pulled off his boots and coat and sat at the table. Gram got him some coffee and the got the sugar bowl and the milk. He smiled at her when she put the stuff by him. "You know I'm not man enough to take it straight don't you?"

Gram's eyes filled with tears and she put her arms around him and hugged him. "You don't need any excuses here you dumb Dane," she whispered in his ear. He put his big arms around her and they both cried for a minute.

Then Gram sat and wiped her eyes. "So," she said, "how about we play a game of cards?"

We all nodded and I got up and got the deck and the cribbage board. For the next three hours we played cribbage. It was one o'clock in the morning and we all were getting very tired.

"I think we should go to bed. They're not going to call any more tonight," Mom said. "Noah, why don't you stay here tonight?"

"I told my family I'd probably stay, so they're not worried," he said.

I kissed Mom and Gram goodnight and Noah and I went upstairs, undressed and got into my bed. Kate climbed up between us and settled down. Noah hugged the old dog. "Kate, you're quite a girl, you know that?"

Kate's tail thumped the bed. He kissed her on the nose and looked over at me. "I think he'll be ok," he said.

"Me too," I said.

"You want to pray?"

I nodded. We both closed our eyes and said a silent prayer. Then Noah reached over and hugged me. "It'll be ok, don't worry."

I lay there for a long time in the dark looking at the ceiling and listening to my best friend's slow breathing. In all of my life I never thought I'd see a dead person and I'd seen two today. I'd never thought about my Mom or Dad dying, especially when I was still a teenager and it was a distinct possibility that that may have happened today too. It was a lot to process.

Kate began to whine and yelp. I looked at her and her toes were wiggling like she was running in her sleep. She must have been dreaming. I put my hand on her back and petted her slowly. "It's ok Kate," I whispered. "It'll all be ok."

CHAPTER 44

I WOKE AT THE SOUND OF THE PHONE ringing downstairs. I heard Mom answer it and then it came back to me that my Dad's ship had been lost in the storm on Monday. Noah stirred and looked at me. "What time is it?" he asked yawning.

I looked at the clock. "It's almost nine," I said.

Just then Gram called up from the bottom of the stairs. "Sebastian, come down here quickly."

"Oh God, Noah," I said.

He put his hand on my shoulder. "Come on, I'll go with you."

We got up and put on our pants and went down the stairs shirtless and barefoot. Mom was crying and talking to someone on the phone. My heart sank.

Gram looked at me and smiled.

"It's your Dad, he's alive," she said.

I grabbed Gram and hugged her. "Are you sure?"

"Yes, I answered the phone, I'm sure," the old woman said beaming. I picked her up and swung her around the room and Noah laughed and clapped his hands.

Just then Mom handed me the phone. "Your Dad wants to talk to you," she said wiping tears from her eyes. She hugged Noah and Gram and they sat and listened.

I grabbed the phone and said, "Dad is that you?"

Dad said, "Sebastian, it's me, I'm ok."

I thought my heart would burst. "Dad, oh man, you can't know how worried we were. How did you...what happened?"

Dad laughed. "I'm sorry kiddo. I had no way to get a message to you. The *Novadoc* ran aground about 7:00 Monday night and she broke in half. The electrical lines and communication lines were cut and the waves were huge so we had to take shelter in the forward cabin with the captain. About half of the guys were in the aft cabin and we had to ride out the storm on separate ends of the ship. The Coast Guard wouldn't come out, the waves were too big and they knew they couldn't get to us, so we just hung on until a fishing boat came and rescued us this morning. We burned furniture to keep warm and it was a pretty miserable night but we all made it except for two of our hands. We lost our old cook, Tony. This was his last voyage. He was going to open a restaurant and retire from the sea. His replacement was a kid not much older than you. We lost him too. Dang nice kid, I feel terrible to think he's gone. They were both washed over the side by a wave that was at least 20 feet high."

"Oh Dad, that's really sad but I'm so glad you made it through. We thought you were gone."

"No, I'm still here and I'll be home in a few days. Right now the Coast Guard wants us to hang around while they investigate and then I'll catch a train to La Crosse. I'll call when I know I'll be arriving and let you know. I don't suppose there's much traffic on the roads yet until all the snow is cleared away.

"You guys had the good sense to get off the river before the storm hit I guess?"

"Oh, well, that's a pretty long story Dad," I said.

Then I began to tell him about our ordeal on the river and the bodies we'd seen on the way back.

"I'm glad you had that solid blind to shelter yourself in," he said. "I wish you'd have been a little more careful when the storm hit but I can understand."

"Dad, if you'd seen all the ducks flying you'd know why it was easy for us to stay too long."

"Didn't old Harry warn you about the storm?"

Suddenly I realized we'd forgotten all about Harry. When we heard about Dad, Harry was forgotten. "We haven't seen Harry since, but we're sure he got off in time. He is one smart old duck hunter," I said.

"You guys better go check on him. He seems to have taken a liking to you. He probably could use some help shoveling out and such."

Dad and I talked for a bit longer and then Mom took the phone. Gram was frying bacon and Noah was standing there grinning. He hugged me when I turned to him. "Wow, what a day," he said.

"No kidding, I'll never forget this day."

Noah said, "We need to go and see if Harry is ok, don't we?"

I nodded. "As soon as Mom is off the phone we'll call Marco and Julio and then we'll go and see Harry."

We got dressed and ate breakfast. After breakfast Noah and I dressed in our heavy clothes and boots and headed toward town walking in the street. We met Marco and Julio where Harry's lane met the main road. The snow plow was just coming back from plowing down to the end of Harry's road. We waved to the driver and he stopped.

"Did you see Harry down there?"

The guy shook his head. "No sign of him. There wasn't any smoke coming from his chimney either."

We looked at each other and we all were worried. "Come on, let's go," I said.

We began to walk down the road and in a bit we began to jog. It only took a few minutes and we reached Harry's cabin. It was dark and there wasn't a track from a dog or man anywhere around it. Julio waded through the deep snow to the boat dock and called back, "His boat isn't here."

"Let's check inside to be sure," I said.

We waded up Harry's sidewalk to the porch and tried the door. It was unlocked as usual and we walked in. "Harry! Harry!"

The only sound was from Harry's grandfather clock ticking. "He's not here," I said with a sense of foreboding.

"Do you think he's...out there?" Noah said looking at the river.

"We've got to go and see," I said.

We hurried out the door and back to town.

CHAPTER 45

WE GOT TO NOAH'S HOUSE half an hour later after walking the streets back to our end of town. Steffen was in the fish house and we walked in. "Dad, we need to take the big boat out again," Noah said.

"Out where? On the river?"

"Yeah, Harry isn't home. His boat's not at this dock."

"Harry would know enough not to stay out in that storm. He must be staying someplace with friends."

"Dad we've got to see. He's been such a good friend to us. What if he's out there stranded?"

"Of course, take the boat. But go easy and be careful. We got you guys back from the storm. We don't want to lose you by having you drown now."

We gassed up the boat and shoved off. The channels were pretty ice free because of the Sheriff boats and other boats going back and forth rescuing people and retrieving bodies. We worked our way out into the marsh and once we got upriver a little way we looked for Harry's tree.

"There," Marco said pointing.

We pushed the boat through the ice and water as close as we could get to the tree. Finally the ice was too thick and we were afraid we'd puncture the hull so we pulled up on the frozen marsh and got out. "We can walk from here," I said.

We started out single file across the marsh toward the tree. The snow was almost hip deep and it was hard going. The marsh was mostly frozen hard but every now and then we'd hit a spot where there must have been a spring and we'd step through to water. We took turns leading. The leader had to stomp down the snow and grass and it was exhausting. It took half an hour to get there but we finally came to Harry's pond.

We stood there trying to catch our breath after the hard hike.

Everything looked so different now covered in snow. There were big drifts piled up behind the muskrat houses.

"Nothing," Julio said.

The pond itself was solid ice and there wasn't much snow on top of the ice because the wind had kept it blown free. We could see little bumps in the snow and we brushed them off and Harry's decoys were sitting there frozen in the ice.

We stood up and looked all around and then I saw a hump in the snow just below the tree. "Guys," I said and motioned toward the hump.

I think we all knew what we'd find and none of us wanted to go look, but we had to. We walked up to the hump and brushed away the snow and it was Harry's boat. It was upside down. We cleared the snow away and found the edge. We scraped the ice and snow from the sides of the boat and all four of us got on one side and grabbed the edge.

"On three," I said.

I counted to three and we all lifted. The boat moved a little and then the ice cracked around the edge and it came up. Harry was lying on his side with his arms around Bea. They were both frozen.

We all stood there looking at our friend. How could this be? He was probably the most knowledgeable duck hunter on the Mississippi river that day and he'd got caught in the storm and it cost him his life.

"I can't believe it," Noah said, tears welling up in his eyes.

I put my arm around his shoulders and we all stood there and had a good cry.

Afterward we decided we had to take him back with us, so we cleaned off the snow from his boat and turned it over right side up. We lifted Harry and Bea up together. They were stiff and there was no way to get Harry's arms from around the old dog. We put them in the bottom of the boat.

"Look, there's his gun," Marco said, stooping to retrieve Harry's old shotgun. He gently laid the gun in the boat and he and Julio took the rope on the bow and pulled and Noah and I pushed from behind. We followed our path we'd made hiking in to the pond and pulled Harry and Bea back with us. It took us a while but we got back to our boat. We left Harry and Bea in their boat and tied it to the back of our boat and started home.

No one said a word on the way back.

When we got to the fish market we tied up the big boat and pulled Harry's boat up onto the land. Noah went inside and told his dad what we'd found. Steffen called the Sheriff. He came out a few minutes later. "He'll bring the ambulance down," he said

Steffen walked over and looked down at Harry. He had a sad smile on his face when he turned back to us. "I know this sounds strange, but I've known Harry for a long time. If Harry had to go, that's the way he would have wanted it......shooting at ducks on one of the most amazing hunting days in history. It's kind of fitting I think."

We all nodded. It was probably just the way Harry would like to go. I could imagine Harry adding this story to all of his great hunting yarns. But it didn't make it any easier for us to lose our friend.

The ambulance drove up and two guys from the Sheriff's dept. loaded Harry and Bea up. We agreed to stop at the office and give him our statement and then they pulled away.

We stood there watching the ambulance disappear up the hill. "Well, what now?" Noah said.

"I don't know about you guys," Marco said, "but I'm going to church and say a prayer for Harry."

That sounded like a good idea and the four of us walked up the hill together.

CHAPTER 46

SCHOOL OPENED again on Wednesday. They finally had enough roads cleared that buses could get kids to the school. We were in gym class and playing basketball without a lot of enthusiasm when the principal came into the gym. He walked up to our teacher and said something to him and motioned for Noah and me to follow him. We thought we probably had done something wrong but when we got outside the gym he told us there was someone there to see us.

When we got to the principal's office Julio was sitting there looking confused and a bit scared. "What did we do?" he asked.

"Nothing boys, there is a man coming who asked to see you boys concerning a matter of importance. He should be here any minute."

Just then his phone rang and he picked it up and said, "Send him right in."

An older man in a fancy suit came into the room and we all stood up.

"Boys, this Judge Murphy. He has some news for you.

The man smiled at us and said to sit down. "Boys, I'm an old friend of Harry Gillette's. Harry and I hunted ducks together for 30 years. I retired from the swamp some years back due to bad knees but Harry and I continued our friendship. I've been his personal attorney for many years."

We sat and listened and wondered where this was going.

"Harry had no family. His wife died many years ago and his only son died quite young. A few weeks ago Harry came to see me and told me he had cancer. It was in his liver and there was nothing the doctors could do for him. And he was over 80 years old, so there wasn't much sense in trying to prolong his life. He came to me and had me make out his will."

We were getting more confused as he talked. What did all this have to do with us?

"Harry wasn't fabulously wealthy but he was comfortable. As a young man he made a good deal of money in railroad stock so he lived quite comfortably all his life. He had a fair amount of money in the bank and some stocks and bonds and of course the cabin. He also had a gun collection that I would expect is worth quite a lot of money. What I'm getting at is that Harry made his will out and named you three, his beneficiaries." He looked at Noah, Julio and me.

"What do you mean?" Noah asked.

"I mean that tomorrow I'll go to the County Courthouse and file this will. Then I'll have the deed to Harry's property and cabin made out into your names. Then I'll put your names on all of his stocks and bonds and accounts and you three will then own Harry's cabin and all of his earthly possessions."

We sat there dumbfounded. "We, we, what?"

Judge Murphy smiled. "Harry told me of your meeting and your passion for the marsh and the outdoors. He thought you guys would enjoy the cabin and maybe could use his money for college or whatever you choose."

The principal smiled at us. "If you guys want to take a minute we can leave you alone," he said.

He and Judge Murphy left and we sat there looking stunned.

"Harry knew he didn't have much time left and he chose to meet his end on the river instead of in a hospital," Noah said sadly.

"I can understand it I guess," Julio said, "but it doesn't make it any easier to lose him."

I turned to Noah and Julio. "I think Marco should be part of this," I said.

They both nodded in agreement. "I thought that first thing," Noah said. "Julio go get your brother, will you?"

Julio went out and asked the principal if he could get Marco and a few minutes later they came into the room. We told Marco of what we'd been told and he was very happy for us "I hope you'll forget all the stupid stuff I did before and let me visit your cabin now and then."

Noah nodded. "No problem Marco, I think living through that storm together kind of bonds us for life."

"Marco we've talked it over and we want you as a partner in the cabin and a part of Harry's will. He'd be happy to have you share in it, I'm sure."

"You guys don't have to do that," I wasn't part of it except for getting lucky enough to spend the night naked in your blind."

We all broke out laughing.

"Well despite seeing you naked, we still want you as a partner in Harry's will," I said.

"Wow, I don't know what to say, but I guess thanks is due," Marco said. Then he hugged each of us.

When Judge Murphy and our principal came back in the room we told the Judge our decision and he agreed to it.

"There's one last thing. Harry wanted to be cremated and he wants you guys to pick the spot to scatter his ashes."

"We know right were that is," I said.

We asked the Judge to have Bea cremated along with Harry and when it was done to let us know. We thanked him and walked back to our classes but the rest of the day was a waste of time for all of us.

After school the four of us walked down the road to Harry's cabin, or I guess to our cabin. The Judge had given us a key to the front door and we opened it and walked in. It was just as it had been the last time we were there except there was no Harry. We really didn't want to look through stuff feeling a little odd at being here but we began to look around and Harry had a lot of cool stuff.

"Where do you suppose he kept his gun collection?" Julio asked.

I looked at the key ring and there was a small brass key on it. "Maybe wherever this key fits," I said.

We went from room to room looking for a cabinet full of guns but found nothing. Then I noticed a door that I'd never been through before. There was a heavy lock on it and I motioned to the guys. I tried the key and the lock turned. When I pushed on the door it felt very heavy.

Noah looked at the door from the edge. "This door has steel inside between the layers of wood. It's like a big safe door."

We pushed the door open and turned on the light. The room was small, maybe ten feet square and there were no windows in it. The walls were made of cement blocks painted white. There were guns everywhere. Gun cabinets stood full, gun racks were filled and hanging from every wall. There was a cabinet with drawers that was full of pistols and handguns.

"My God, you could start a war with all of these," Marco said.

"These have to be worth a small fortune," I said.

Noah grinned. "Harry told us he collected a lot of stuff. I never thought he meant hundreds of guns."

Harry was just full of surprises I guess.

CHAPTER 47

IN THE DAYS AND WEEKS after the storm we came to realize just what we'd managed to live though. The storm had claimed many lives in Minnesota and on through Wisconsin and then across Lake Michigan. No one was prepared for a storm of such ferocity and it caught hundreds of people in situations that cost them their lives.

On Lake Michigan three ships sank. The *Anna C. Minch* and the *William B. Davok* were lost with all hands. The *Novadoc,* my Dad's ship managed to break apart on a reef and they only lost their two cooks who were swept off the deck by a huge wave. In total 66 sailors perished in the cold waters of Lake Michigan. Thankfully my dad was one who survived.

People died through the area when they got stalled in cars and were buried by the snow. Two people died when two trains going the opposite way on the tracks collided. One of the trains missed seeing a signal because of the snow.

There was a story of three men who got stranded and tried to walk to safety. They hiked through the snow but visibility was nearly zero. They were desperate to find shelter because they weren't dressed warm enough for the terrible winds and frigid temperatures. Finally they found a culvert under the road and crawled into it to get out of the wind. They found them frozen inside the culvert after the storm, just 100 feet from a house that they couldn't see.

The day was deadly for duck hunters. In addition to our dear friend Harry, 48 other hunters either drown trying to get back to shore in their little duck boats or froze to death, stranded on the islands of the Mississippi river. Many like Harry had tried to wait out the storm under their boats with their faithful hunting dogs. Some managed to light fires that they kept burning all night. We saw one of those fires miles away and it turned out that those hunters survived. Most weren't as lucky as we had been to have a big solid blind that saved our lives. We didn't have an inkling that our blind would ever be anything more than a fun place for us to hunt in luxury. Little did we know when we built the thing that it would be our salvation in the great storm.

In all 145 people died and countless cattle, poultry and other animals succumbed to the snow and cold. Over a million Thanksgiving turkeys froze to death in Minnesota.

About a week after the storm Judge Murphy had a box delivered to my house with two urns inside. One held Harry's ashes and the other Bea's. I called the other guys and the four of us met and went to Harry's cabin. The cabin was now our cabin but Harry was always present with us in spirit. We met to talk over what to do with the ashes.

"First, I want to propose that we keep this place as our hunting and fishing cabin forever," I said. "If we move away, we'll still own it and come back when we can to use it. I also think it should be called Harry's Cabin."

There was no discussion about selling it or any of the stuff we'd inherited from Harry. When one of us died someday our families would inherit our share.

Everyone agreed and we sealed it with a handshake all around.

"What about Harry and Bea," Noah said.

"I've been thinking of the right place for them and I think we should take them out where they died, on Harry's Pond. Let's leave them under the tree where they spent so many hours of enjoyment," Julio said.

We all agreed that was an excellent idea. The problem was that it the river was now frozen solid and there was no way to get out there.

"We'll just have to wait until spring," Marco suggested.

So, we put the urns on the fireplace mantle and there they stayed until the river thawed in April.

In the meantime we built some bunk beds in the cabin and arranged things more to our liking. We took an inventory of the gun room and found Harry had indeed liked to collect guns. There were nearly 200 of them. We decided to keep them and just use them. Now and then we heard of someone having tough times we'd give them one or two to help them out. If we heard of a family that had kids who were hunting age but not able to afford a gun we'd give them what they needed.

We'd lost the decoys at our blind and Harry's had also been lost but we still had over 250 hand carved wooden decoys in the shed. As we would soon find out, some of those decoys were worth a lot of money. As far as hunting and fishing gear went, we were set for life.

We all piled into the big boat one spring day after the winter finally was over and went out the channel and up river to Harry's Pond. The ice was gone and the bulrushes were just beginning to sprout up on the land. There were red winged black birds singing their spring mating songs and many ducks flying over the marsh sporting their spring plumage.

We pulled up next to the tree and got out. Marco and Noah lifted a slab of marble out of the bottom of the boat and we stood it against the tree. We'd gotten it from the local tombstone man. It was just a simple piece of rough marble, kind of dark brown mud color and on the front of it was carved, *Harry and Bea, November 11, 1940.*

I took a shovel and dug a shallow hole just deep enough to lay the two canisters on their sides in the wet soil. Noah and Marco laid the stone over it and we stood back and looked down on the final resting place of our friend and his old dog.

It was silent and the breeze was blowing and we all looked up and smiled at each other. Noah and Julio went to the boat and came back with four shotguns. Noah loaded one shell into each of them and we each took a gun. We stood side by side and aimed out over the marsh and fired one time.

The birds and ducks in the area flew up into the sky, startled by the shot. We watched them circle back and settle in.

"I think Harry'll be at peace here," I said.

Each of us took a turn and stooped down, touched the stone and said a final goodbye to Harry and then we got back into the boat. Noah fired up the motor and we left Harry's Pond behind us.

Present Day

THE FOUR OF US SPENT COUNTLESS HOURS in Harry's Cabin over the next years. We built a larger boat dock and made more room for fishing. After we were out of high school and working we built a barbecue on the river bank and had many great parties with our girlfriends and later our wives and children.

Kate died at age 14 and we buried her ashes with Harry and Bea. Little Karen lived to be 19. She loved the cabin and spent hours there with us just being a dog. When she died we lay her ashes with those of her old friend Kate.

As our families grew we built an addition on the cabin and turned it into a bunk house. We had room for a dozen people to sleep in the extra room in several sets of bunk beds.

We hunted from our blind for years and years. The tree was solid and the blind was built to last. What finally got it was a barge. A big tug boat pushing ten huge steel barges loaded with grain lost their direction in the dark one summer night and slammed into the blind turning it into kindling. We didn't find out until many weeks later when the four of us were out fishing.

"Holy crap, what the heck happened to it?" Marco said looking shocked.

"Looks like somebody blew it up," I said.

We got out on the bank and then when we got closer we could see the big gouge in the bank of the island where the bow of the barge had slammed through the blind and into the island.

"The barge captain probably never even knew he smashed it," Noah said.

It was pretty sad to see our great blind destroyed but it had served its purpose for many years and we'd had countless hours of fun in it. It had also saved our lives.

190

Noah went into his Dad's business and ran the fish market for his whole life. Julio did the same with his Dad's fish business and they were friendly rivals for many years, and then they decided to merge their two businesses and they became one of the largest fish producers in the country.

I went into the sporting goods business and had a successful store specializing in firearms and duck hunting supplies. After seeing all the different types of gear that one could amass I thought it was a business I'd enjoy and that would be profitable. I had a great time until I retired and my son took over for me.

Marco surprised us all when he announced he was going to enter the Seminary and become a Priest. We hadn't seen that one coming. When we asked him about it he told us that he felt that God had given him a second chance that day on the river when he'd nearly died and he wanted to devote his life to helping others. He was ordained and made the assistant pastor at a church in nearby La Crosse. He still spent many weekends with us hunting and fishing and having a few beers together. When he was in his "civilian" clothes and out hunting with us he was just Marco as he'd always been. When he was conducting Mass or a baptism he was Father Marco. In 1951 when the Korean conflict broke out, he enlisted in the army and went to war as a chaplain. He was killed in 1952 when a plane he was in was hit by enemy fire and crashed in a fireball.

We were all terribly saddened by the loss of Marco. His body burned up but the army sent his dog tags home. His mother let us have the dog tags and we added them under the stone on Harry's Pond, next to Harry and the dog's ashes.

Noah, Julio and I used the cabin almost every week until a short while ago when Julio's son came driving up one evening when we were planning on bluegill fishing and told us Julio had been in an accident. Noah and I rushed to the hospital. Julio's wife and several of his kids were gathered around his bed. He was sleeping and we talked to his wife but the news was not good. He'd been crushed and had internal injuries that were not repairable. As we were talking Julio opened his eyes and smiled at us all. He took his wife's hand and she kissed him. Then he looked at Noah and me and nodded his head and winked. "The pond," he whispered, and he was gone.

His family knew of our close bond and Harry's Pond and his wife asked us to take his ashes there so he'd be in a place that he loved so much. After his funeral she gave us his urn and asked us to take him to the river.

Today Noah and I are taking Julio's ashes out to Harry's Pond where we'll all be one day. We're old men like Harry was when we knew him. We've made arrangements that when the last one of us goes, we'll be taken and laid to rest with the others. Noah still runs the outboard and knows the twists and turns of the river. We go a little slower than we used to go and are a little more careful. We pulled into the pond and up on shore by the tree which is now a very large maple. I got out and held the boat for Noah. His knees aren't what they once were. Neither of us is as spry as we once were. Noah climbed out and brought the canister with Julio's ashes in it.

We stood there looking over the pond. It was a tiny little place that was as beautiful to someone who loved the marsh as any place on earth. The breeze was blowing and the cattails were swaying. A red winged black bird sang its jolly little song.

"This is a great place to end up," Noah said.

"Yeah, I sure could think of worse places."

It was a struggle to lift the slab of granite but we got it up and laid Julio next to his brother's dog tags and our friend Harry and our old dogs. We let the stone back down and Noah looked at me.

"That's where we'll be one of these days."

"Yeah, I guess we will," I said. "It'll be good for us all to be together again."

I lifted two shotguns out of the boat and we slid one shell into each of them. We stood side by side and aimed out over the pond and fired a salute to our friends.

In Memory of Katy

In memory of my
golden retriever Katy.
I'll miss her.

About the Author

Dan Bomkamp has made his home in the Wisconsin River valley all his life with the exception of his college years in La Crosse. He has been an avid hunter and fisherman his whole life. For many years he was in the sporting goods industry and began writing in the 80's for outdoor magazines. He is active in the Foreign Exchange Student program having hosted 33 boys from 13 countries over the years. Golden Retrievers have also been a big part of his life. He had at least one Golden sharing his home for 33 years. He lives in Muscoda with his cat Tigger.

His previous books are: *The Adventures of Thunderfoot; More Adventures of Thunderfoot; Thanks Thunderfoot; The Best of Thunderfoot; The Gosey; Big Edna—Back to the Gosey; Voyageur; Lost Flight; Tag.*

Check out his website at www.danbomkamp.com
Or you can email him at danbomkamp@live.com